ENTERTAINING SALLY ANN

by
Robert Nisbet

ALUN BOOKS
3 Crown Street, Port Talbot

© Robert Nisbet 1997
ISBN 0 907117 75 9

ACKNOWLEDGEMENTS

Some of these stories first appeared in the following magazines:
The New Welsh Review, The Cardiff Poet, Momentum, Cambrensis and *SWAGMAG*.
"The Maid of the Mountains" appeared in Romania in the anthology *THE TIME TRAVELLER* (Porto Franco Publishing).

Cover design by Derilynn Fitzgerald

Printed in Great Britain by
C. I. Thomas & Sons (Haverfordwest) Ltd., Press Buildings, Merlins Bridge, Haverfordwest

To my readers

To Carole,

with warmest good wishes,

Peter Nixon.

20. xi. 98

BIOGRAPHICAL NOTE

ROBERT NISBET was born in Haverfordwest and now lives, writes and teaches in that area. His previous collections of short stories include *Sounds of the Town* (a runner-up in the Dylan Thomas Award competition in 1983), *Downmarket* and *The Ladybird Room*. Many of his stories have been published in the U.S.A., Germany and Romania, broadcast on BBC radio and included in a WJEC study pack for GCSE students. He has also written poems, radio scripts, plays for voices, and hundreds of articles and reviews.

He has been, part-time and at various times, President of Debates in the University of Essex, resident raconteur in the Haverfordwest folk club, a regular broadcaster on the Radio Wales series *Sunday Best*, a theatre critic for *The Western Mail*, and director of the literary performance group, the Yorick Players. He has given readings of his stories in numerous arts festivals, colleges and pub gigs, and is a founder member of the reading group West of Whitland Poets.

ENTERTAINING SALLY ANN

Contents

THE HUSH AND WASH OF NIGHT

c/o Beynon,
12 Rossetti Avenue,
Haverfordwest
28th August 1990

Dear Watkyn,

Warmest greetings from my new digs in Poets' Corner. It's not the same, not as good, as the last three years with you and Gweno, of course. A corner shop in a valleys village really did have it all for an aspirant storyteller, as you well know. But I have hopes of Harfat too — and Poets' Corner.

I haven't fully cased the town yet, but I don't need to. In my very digs themselves there is much matter for the satirical mind. For I am lodging, Watkyn, with a Mr. and Mrs. Fart and their son Hamlet, and you, with your keen eye for a social misfit, would relish this unlikely entourage. Let me fill you in.

Both "Mr. and Mrs. Fart" and "Hamlet" are, as you'll have guessed, nicknames of my own devising. You'll have deduced from my address that their real name is Beynon. But a fart is a fart, Watkyn, apprehend him how you will, and Mr. B. really is the biggest old fart you'd encounter in the breadth of South Wales. I shall of course need to give him a Christian name as well — so I think I'll call him "Shortarse". He's a little round hogshead of a man, with round thick specs and a shiny bald head.

And really, Watkyn, he *is* useless. He's awful. He sits and moans and pontificates, the man with all the answers. We were watching the European athletics on television last night, and his son Hamlet (of whom more shortly) was urging some British boy on to a bronze medal. "O-ho," says Shortarse — and he has an odd little verbal habit, a rising note with a gurgle in the middle. "O-ho," says he, "o-ho no. No bloody fear. Bugger your bronze. Stuff that. It's gold for me or nothing. I'm a gold medal man."

Now that I find truly amazing. This great fat useless lump, who hasn't been off his backside for decades, putting the world to rights from the sagging depths of his armchair. He really is phenomenal. He'll look round drily at every snag and hitch, and find

7

fault. Constantly. He'll read of the salaries of television perform-ers and moan. "O-ho, yes, all on the licence fee, I dare say." And thus from hour to hour he sits and stews.

His son Hamlet takes a fair amount of stick. I call him "Hamlet" because he's usually dressed in black, a black-clad beat with long black hair who mopes and moons around the house some nights, and oftentimes retires to his bedroom, ostensibly to play his Guns 'n' Roses tapes, more possibly, I suspect, to brood. And, let's face it, if you had Shortarse for your old man, you'd have something to brood about.

Hamlet is seventeen. He's in school, doing his 'A' levels this year, and it could conceivably be that there is some shape to the boy. He tells me he's doing art in school, and I've seen a few of his paintings, which aren't at all bad. Perhaps he'll get good 'A' levels, for he does in fact work quite hard, in between bouts of brooding, but this would still be an impressive thing, for he's blessed with a couple of parents who have to open negotiations at the breakfast table as to who's using the family brain cell for the day. And they really do give him stick. It seems there's some mate of Shortarse's, a Councillor Vaughan, who has a son who's doing better in school than Hamlet is, and who used to score more goals in the Cubs football, and God knows what. "O-ho," says Shortarse, "bugger your Cs and Ds. It's As and Bs you want, boy. Billy Vaughan will have the buggers, you watch," and Mrs. Fart — let's call her the Tragedy Queen — sits by and sniffs, in a pointed sort of way, her lips tight and her features frozen into an icy and catarrhal disapproval. "Your father's right, Brian" ("Brian" being Hamlet's real name). "Your father's right. I'm sure that Billy Vaughan won't settle for less. You'll need to get your head down." And, as I say, the poor kid does work quite hard.

And thus he broods — and wouldn't you? So there you go, Watkyn. That's my new digs. I start my spruce new teaching career on Monday — but not in Hamlet's school, thank God. Meantime, I'll keep on chipping out the stories down this end. There are characters here a-plenty, as you'll have gathered. I'll write again. Keep in touch.

All the best
Steve

c/o Beynon,
12 Rossetti Avenue,
Haverfordwest
19th October 1990

Dear Watkyn,

A long overdue bulletin from the Fart front. I should by now tell you news of the town and the school and reassure you that I'm firing on all fronts, but I find it hard to get any news bulletin beyond the front door of 12 Rossetti Avenue. Honestly, Watkyn, these Beynons are amazing.

I told you last time of my young friend "Hamlet". Well, for a start, can I call that nickname in? I'd like to re-christen him "Lodovico". Do you remember that Eliot poem we liked, the Alfred Prufrock one? We recited chunks of it back and fore one night at the snooker, when the guest celebrity (Reardon, I think) was late arriving. Well, that's Lodovico precisely: "am not Prince Hamlet nor was meant to be. Am an attendant lord, one that will do to swell a progress, start a scene or two". You'll recall the passage.

And that's Lodovico. That's our man. He has a quite uncanny ability for coming second at *everything*. And I mean, everything. It's a gift he has. Years ago, so the Tragedy Queen assures me, he was second highest goalscorer in the Cubs team, behind the boy Billy Vaughan. He's just got a Highly Commended in a schools' art competition. He came in second in three events in last year's school sports. He's on the reserve list for some crowd of youngsters who are being lined up to meet the Princess Royal. He goes fishing quite often and catches medium sized fish. And next summer he should get moderately good 'A' levels before ambling off to a good second-tier art college. He really is one of life's silver medallists — or not quite that, really. He's the sort of bloke who'll surprise everyone by reaching the final, and then come in a respectable fourth or fifth.

Now Lodovico is in fact what they call in the valleys "a tidy old boy". I find him quiet, but he paints, plays football, writes history essays — I've known him go to the theatre. His problem, dear Brutus, is not in himself, but in his old man. For if Lodovico is the archetypal runner-up, Shortarse is the archetypal loudmouth in the stand, the apotheosis of the armchair critic. Every time Lodovico comes in second, Shortarse is crabbing. "O-ho, that's no bloody good. It's guts you want boy, guts and application." I think he works on the principle that he himself *associates* with the great and good. He sees them on television. He reads about them in the *Sun*, and he thinks that if he comments in a loud voice, "That's my boy. Lineker's your man," or, "It's Princess Di for me, boy," he accumulates some portion of their glory. Thereupon he is in a position to nag at Lodovico anew with his own impressive armoury of tautological abuse. "O-ho no. It's goals in the back of the net that count, boy. Any bugger can have shots blocked on the line."

The Tragedy Queen has, if anything, an even nastier line in invective. She'll follow Lodovico's affairs at first hand even: she'll go to art exhibitions and watch the odd football match, and then make comments. Sniffy ones. "That girl who got first prize, Brian. I don't know, her paintings had something." A weary sigh, and then: "Spirit, I suppose, More *feeling*." As if to say, "Oh God, how sharper than a serpent's tooth it is to have a second-place son."

Maybe, Watkyn, you'll read one day that a Haverfordwest 'A' level student has just taken a meat-axe to his miserable, griping parents. And don't be surprised to read that the family lodger had whetted the axe for him. As I say, he's a tidy old boy who deserves more than this pair of screwballs.

For the rest, school is fine, the people round town are pleasant, and the football team's not bad. They had an away game with Ton last week, and I'd hoped to get up, but didn't. I'll see you some-time, though, surely.

My love to Gweno. All the best
Steve.

*

Dear Watkyn,

I'm sure you'll have appreciated the fact that my two winter letters played down the story of young Lodovico, and pushed him and the grumbling Shortarse into bit parts. You'll forgive me if *this* letter takes up the Lodovico story afresh, for I really have the most bizarre tale to relate.

It all happened two nights ago. Shortarse had been stewing quietly in front of some television quiz show. His tactic on these occasions is to put the sound down on his armchair control (and they invented armchair controls with Shortarse in mind, I fancy) and then to turn it up for the prizes. That way he can associate himself with the winners and their attendant glory, without first having to undergo the embarrassment of not knowing any of the answers. Anyway, he'd just switched on the sound and was gloating over the fact that he'd won a holiday for two in Hawaii, when Lodovico came in, having been to a Karaoke contest in a local pub — and come second. Shortarse was disposed to pass over this mediocrity with a weary groan, but the Tragedy Queen started sniffing and fishing for news. "Who won then, Brian? Was he good?" For God's sake — a Karaoke contest in the Greyhound!

All this seemed to cheese Lodovico off just that little bit more than usual. Generally, he shrugs, broods a little, ships the stick, and eventually wanders off to his bedroom. Often though, he'll go fishing — particularly when the domestic harassment has been more spiteful than usual. This time he snapped it out just a little more sharply. "Okay. I came second. And I enjoyed it." And then, "I'm going fishing down by the quay." Then, to my great surprise, he turned to me. "Do you want to come, Steve?"

Now I thought this was a great idea, and I was flattered to be asked. He has been increasingly communicative lately, and underneath the brooding there's quite a nice and affable side to him. I think maybe he senses I could be an ally of sorts.

So we dug out wellies and thick coats and set off, around eleven that evening, for a spot Lodovico knows just below the quay. But what got me — and it's hard to describe this, Watkyn — was one extraordinary moment just after we left the house.We'd trudged off, not saying much, until we got to the corner of Rossetti Avenue. Then Lodovico turned, looked back, hard and square-on, at his parents' house, fixed it firmly in his sights, and breathed in very deeply and slowly. Then he just said, in a low voice, "Bastard, bastard, bastard!" Then walked on. And he seemed calmer straight away.

Obviously, I didn't know what to say, but after a while he started to confide. In a way, he told me, he regards his parents as a bad joke, and he just wants to get his 'A' levels, get to college and get the hell out of it. But meanwhile, he *enjoys* life, he reckons — he likes the football and the painting and the Karaoke contests and he's had a few girl friends. But hell it would be nice, he thought, if his parents could take it in the same spirit.

I found that quite amazing, but I just had to mumble agreement — and then we were laying out rods on the river bank just below the quay. And that was the next, and really astounding, thing. Again, I don't quite know how to describe it. I've always been an urban animal myself, as you know, and I'd never really been fishing before — but I did enjoy it. We were there till four, and it was dark apart from a little moonlight and a small hand lamp which Lodovico had brought. There was just the lapping of the water, the wind blowing a little — around two, two-thirty, it got up slightly and was moaning and whistling — and then this great hush all around us. Lodovico was in fact fishing very intently, flicking the line out regularly — you'd get the whistle and plop of the line going out, and then the hush again. Twice we did get a small fish, and we had a little excitement — then stillness.

We talked very little, from midnight through till four, but there was no need. For what really staggered me — again, it's hard to describe — was the fact (and I could *sense* it, honestly) that Lodovico was so obviously and utterly *at peace*. He really was. It was all within him, the silence, the darkness, with just the flicker of his lamp and the flick of his line, and that strange hush and wash of the night all around us, and the river lapping. He *wasn't* brooding — he was utterly serene. As we walked back at four, he chatted contentedly — quite relaxed, quite easy, quite charming.

So there you go. Sorry to ramble on so much about the Rossetti

Avenue Mafia, but they really have marked this year for me. School's O.K. — and I've joined the civic society. They have a talk next week on the town's newspapers. Keep in touch, Watkyn. I'll write again soon.

Regards
Steve

*

c/o Beynon,
12 Rossetti Avenue,
Haverfordwest
19th August 1991

Dear Watkyn,

I'm writing in haste to ask you not to send letters to this address again. Tomorrow I'm going out to look for a flat. The sooner I can shake the dust of 12 Rossetti Avenue off my feet, the happier I'll be. It's been bloody here, Watkyn — and you'll have recalled that last Thursday was 'A' level results day.

I'd expected Brian's results to be scrutinised a little critically, but honestly, Watkyn, I wasn't quite prepared for last Thursday's display. Brian got back from school about eleven — I'll call him Brian, by the way — I've lost my taste for nicknames. As I say, he got back about eleven. He'd got respectable grades, a B and two Ds, which isn't bad at all. In fact, that B in Art was pretty good. And the Beynons sniffed around all this for a while, and then snooped for Billy Vaughan's results *He'd* got a B in Art as well (and it was his weakest subject) and an A and a B in the other two.

And the sum total of the response was Mrs. Beynon saying, "Good for Billy Vaughan", and the old man just growling, "Better get your accommodation form off then. They take runners-up in art college, I'm told." Can you believe that? So Brian mooched all day, went down town or something, and in the evening we all sat round saying very little.

Watkyn, I loved my own parents dearly, as you know, and even after the accident, I not only had you and Gweno through those college years, but I had the memories of Mum and Dad — and I

13

always felt and knew that they'd have supported me and sided with me, always. Which is why I can hardly believe that Brian can survive this kind of meanness. Later in the evening, Mrs. B., perhaps as a prelude to a further twist of the knife, announced she was going to ring Billy Vaughan's parents to congratulate them. And then Brian did seem to snap, for a moment. "Sod this," he said, getting up, "I'm going fishing, and sod the two of you." He got his wellies and his tackle, there and then, around ten o'clock, and he was gone.

He didn't invite me this time, understandably, and I just went to bed around midnight — and lay awake, and looked at my watch now and again, and worried. Come four o'clock, I was convinced, I really was, that we'd find him, in the morning, floating in the river, and the Beynons would say they couldn't understand it, because he'd done so well in his 'A' levels, and people would call it "death by misadventure". Jesus wept, Watkyn. That boy's whole life has been one long bloody misadventure.

By four o'clock, I couldn't stand it any more. I dressed and sneaked out, and made my way down to Brian's fishing spot by the quay. And he was there, he was fine, he was — again, I could sense this — he was *at peace*. He nodded to me and then, literally, we said nothing. Just sat, with that same strange hush around us, till dawn. And then we plodded back to Rossetti Avenue, chatting about oddments. He was just as he'd been on the couple of other fishing trips on which I've gone with him: affable, contented... yes, can you believe this, happy.

So what do I say? He won't excel at academic work, or sport, or anything, in any colossal way. There've been odd times I've hoped he might wander away and brood, and catch all of the cruelty in some black and beautiful paintings. That's the real romantic myth, isn't it? But he won't do that either, because even his painting isn't that good. But he will of course go fishing — and sit on river banks at night, and find a peace in that. It's a gift he has, and I can't fully understand it. But it does make him a winner of a kind, and it gives him something his big useless slob of a father will never know or appreciate.

As I say, I'm going to move out now. Brian will cope, I know, but I don't want to be left here after he's gone. It's a funny thing, Watkyn. I feel ashamed now of those early letters I sent you from

14

Poets' Corner, all nicknames and jokes. I'd reckoned I'd be a storyteller and I'd go in search of characters. But sometimes the
characters find *you*, and it's not so simple any more. It hurts.

My love to Gweno — and to yourself
Steve

CARDIFF '64

I sat for an hour or so last night in the Yeoman, through to closing time, talking to a friend, a journalist. Let us call him Gigadibs, after the character in the Browning poem. I won't say that, like the Bishop in that poem, I rolled him out my mind, but it was a lengthy conversation, and he has the journalist's knack of probing. He wasn't interviewing me for anything, he just seemed to want to know, and I told him all of it: Cardiff in 1964, Ron and Larry, the years since: all of it. We'd found our way to the Yeoman after a Male Voice concert, and the conversation had been prompted by a few derisive remarks on my part about my old mate Blackmore, who'd done a solo spot at the concert. And then we got talking.

I don't think I want to trot all this out in what is known, I think, as "conventional story form". In other words, I don't want to report on this as a conversation, and keep breaking off to say things like "asked Gigadibs, shifting his elbow out of a pool of lager" and other extraneous bollocks of that kind. I think it'll help me, as it helped me last night, in making sense to myself of the whole puzzling complex of things, if I report it in a question-and-answer format.

You'll find Gigadibs in italics. I'm the one who says a lot. So here goes...

Why the mockery of Blackmore, then?

Blackmore's a lovely bloke, he's fun, he's a laugh, and he'll do a first rate spot at a male voice concert. But he's a rogue, he really is, he's a con, a charlatan.

Put it this way. Did you notice the programme note? Blackmore, we are told, studied at the Welsh College of Music and Drama. Never happened. Blackmore was up in Cardiff in 1964 on one of his few forays out of town, and there were a lot of the boys from town up in Cardiff just then. And Blackmore was a post office clerk.

Are you bitter about that?

Bitter? Good God, no. The whole con of it, it's such a lovely Blackmore thing, wonderfully in character. We used to meet him in Cardiff, in the Students' Union bar and dances, and he was bullshitting then. If the whole dream I cherish, Cardiff in 1964, is to survive, then Blackmore's lovely feckless bullshit will be a part of that dream.

You've mentioned that Cardiff '64 thing before...

It's a myth, it's a dream. There were quite a lot of boys from town up in Cardiff then, on degrees, teacher training, jobs. And three of us in particular had a flat in Roath. We had girl friends back in town and went back at weekends quite often (and in fact we all married them in time), but we were happily un-engaged and free to roam the bars and dances. Footloose. It was the sort of opening out to life you only get when you're twenty-two. We had all the plans in the world.

Did you reckon you were going places?

Well, yes and no. If you can believe this, we really felt, even then, we were going Harfat. We were, at twenty-two, questing out, yes, but we wanted to go back to town, that was part of it. And I suppose that sounds now like a very tame, safe, soft, unambitious thing to want. But it really didn't seem that way. We were going to go back, go home, in a year or two, but we really were going back in a mood of colour and celebration. It was a looking-forward, joyful thing. We'd head back, in Ron's car, every two or three weeks, and... well, you may not remember the town in the sixties. It had a lovely rambling entry: there was a newsagent's shop hidden away down a flight of steps, a curve, - and then the town, tucked away and huddled round its hill. It was captivating, like a warm surprise to be re-discovered on a Friday night.

But had you any other ambitions?

Sure, we did. I was going to be the writer, as you'll have guessed. I was going to capture it, delineate it, the reality of the thing. You can quarrel with what I've written maybe, but you can't quarrel with the dream.

As for Ron... well. Teaching does sound tame, I realise, but Ron was right into being the inspirational history teacher. He probably wouldn't have thanked me for saying this, but teaching to Ron was a moral thing. A crusade. These were the nineteen sixties, remember, and there wasn't that feeling then that teaching was something you fell back on. Ron was a working class boy come through, and he had... well, two ideals. There were the old grammar school masters he'd admired, and scholarship... Ron had done a stint of research along the way. And then the real sixties liberal humanist thing, the school as a caring community. If you'd told Ron then (or told me or Larry) that teaching was a backwoods, insignificant thing, we wouldn't have worn it.

And Larry?

Now Larry was the surprise. He was the real child of the early sixties, your genuine mad psychologist. Not many Harfats had done degrees in psychology then, and, to be honest, I hadn't fully expected him to come back to town as avidly as Ron and I did. But he found a job in town, as an educational psychologist, in '66 and back he came. But, as I say, he was Cardiff '64, was Larry. He was parties and pubs and Indian curries. I'm sure he loved Gaynor even then, and does to this day, but he seemed to combine a hankering for the weekend trips to town to see her with falling in love about twice a fortnight in Cardiff. And there were skip jive and folk cellars and football matches, and that mad wild-bearded Larry in his sandals, charging down Queen Street after six pints and an Indian, chanting all his old undergraduate bawdries. "Never Mind the Moon, Get 'Em Doon". That kind of thing.

So what happened when you got back to town? Was it as good as you'd expected?

Oddly, no. Or not for just a while. We married, and there were mortgages, and for just two, three years, we were a little uneasy, really. We used to meet once a week in the Yeoman, and we set up a little circle of our own. The phrase "think tank" was just coming into use, as I remember, and we called ourselves "The Sceptic Tank". We used to sit and plot, and pick off local personalities and councillors, and take the piss. Larry wanted to bring out our own broadsheet — he even had a provisional title, "The Cistern", but nothing came of it. Nothing came of that little spell really. It was too forced, I think, too anxious. We wanted to recapture a student past, and hadn't really fitted it to anything.

So what happened? Did you all become middle-aged?

Not really. The great thing was that if we did become middle-aged, we didn't really notice. As I say, we got into things. You see, I mentioned our girl friends, wives as they became. Well, by great good fortune, they all of them seemed to have the nous to realise that there's a part of many a man which is always a small boy. And, the big thing, we all had sons, of around the same age.

And after a while, after the Sceptic Tank had died the death, other things started to move. I placed a few stories, not many, but enough to make me feel I'd kept a promise. And Ron and Larry were really into their jobs. By the time Ron was thirty, thirty-five, he really had a name as a teacher, believe me. Society may be into mediamen and executives, but the "gifted history teacher" tag still carries some clout.

And Larry was a revelation in a way. He was never the ideal employee, I shouldn't have thought, because he was very impatient of red tape and very indiscreet, but he did sometimes get very involved — too much so perhaps for a psychologist. Larry's job involved him quite often with problem kids and took him into homes and schools. He'd end up very often taking the kid's side and this didn't always endear him to head teachers. There was also the time he had a fight with a parent, down in Pembroke Dock. And then, in the Yeoman on a Friday, we'd get the full blast of Larry's sense of outrage.

I suppose Ron and Larry were both very committed to their jobs, in their way. I maybe less so — I moved from journalist to information officer after a few years — but then of course my main thrust was always writing.

What about your sons?

Well, that was the best part, really, that united us. We had Cubs football matches and family things and we didn't notice at the time the way the old moods were being re-directed. Larry would go berserk at Cubs football. He still had the wild shock of beard and his duffel coat and he'd let it go. "There is no way Neyland will pull back three. Bury them, boys. Bury the bastards!" And other parents would complain, of course, but Larry has always been Larry. And Ron meanwhile took over as coach of the team. Yes, we got involved with parental things.

Then?

Male Voice. Cricket. Football. Basically we watched football and played cricket. None of us was much good, but we spread ourselves around the third and fourth elevens, and roamed the county, playing in villages like Llechryd and St. Florence. I used to go round the young farmers' clubs, coaching them for drama competitions. Sometimes the six of us would get together, with the kids, and go to cricket matches in Swansea. And there was

Guy Fawkes Night. Then, in time, our sons joined the cricket club. And none of us, ever, stood for the council. They were good days.

"Were?"

Ron died about two years ago. Cancer. It's a strange thought. When we were in Cardiff, we didn't really believe in things like cancer. Or death, really. It was never really talked about, except in health and smoking campaigns, so, yes, we knew about it, we believed in it — but not really. Not deep down.

And Larry? He's all right?

Well. Bouts of angina, and he's taken early retirement, but he's bubbling around as well as ever now. Yes, Larry's pretty good. He thinks now he will bring out that broadsheet called "The Cistern".

So have you any regrets?

Regrets maybe, but not always the obvious ones. There have been illness and death to contend with, and those are scars, real scars, but in a way it is possible to come to terms with that kind of grief. I'm surprised sometimes to find that the real grief goes deeper, for it should only be a regret. It's the loss of the callowness, I think, the innocence. What happened to Larry, and to Ron in particular, in the end, I can accept, for there was so much in between: parenthood, pubs, and cricket and companionship. Above all, perhaps, there was middle-aged marital love, and that surely must be the most unforeseen and underestimated phenomenon of them all. But before that: as I say, there were the innocence, the expectancy, life as a story, to be speculated upon and guessed at.

Cardiff in '64 was the promise, the yearning, life thereafter the prolonged coitus. There is something absolute about the longings and desires of late adolescence, and Cardiff was a sudden rush of optimism and speculative joy. We travelled so hopefully and so naively, and the future beckoned. I've enjoyed all of it, but still, somehow, something is always lost — and I can see no obvious reason why.

MAGIC

c/o Beynon,
12 Rossetti Avenue,
Haverfordwest
14th November 1990

Dear Watkyn,

Okay. I've settled into my new digs (as I've told you) and the job in school (as I've told you also). More now on this little town itself. I like it — I really do. It's homely and cheerful. But — see what you make of this, Watkyn. There are undercurrents.

Let me start with a little story told me by some old boy a few weeks back. (I say "old boy" — was about your age — fiftyish.) Anyway, he told me of how he went to a wrestling tournament in the town around 1960. There was a coloured boy in one of the bouts, and in those days virtually no-one in the town had ever met or seen a Negro. So, the bout proceeded, but at the end the M.C., complete with dickybow and dinner jacket, got up to say he had been shocked to hear, during the preceding bout, someone refer to one of the wrestlers as "Sambo". He wasn't sure that he hadn't even heard the word "nigger". Now he was sure we were all sportsmen and gentlemen in Haverfordwest, and this was sullying the good name of the town, and so forth...

How quaint, you will say, but that was 1960. But we're thirty years on now, Watkyn, there *are* a few coloured people around the town, mainly black Americans from the naval base at Brawdy, but I do wonder which way the town is heading. Let me give you this latest news bulletin, and you can judge for yourself.

As I've told you, I've been supporting the town's football club. It's an odd set-up, in a way, because the whole side is bought in from Swansea, a bunch of Swansea Jack semi-pros, who even train in the Afan Lido in Port Talbot, I gather. But they're supported to the hilt by a crowd of the gnarled, weather-beaten old boys who are everywhere in the town, and there's a real affection here for "the Swansea boys". Added to which, they're a good side, well up in the Welsh League, as you know, and they play some lovely one-touch football. (Give them a good goalscorer up front, we reckon, and they could win the League).

Anyway. They had a home game with Margam a fortnight or so back, and out, in the Margam strip,there loped a tall and rangy coloured boy, something you see from time to time in clubs to the East. He was a super player, quick, graceful, cool, and was constantly referred to, by his team mates, as "Magic". Once, when he stumbled over a ball, there was some grouchy voice at the back of our stand saying, "Magic, my arse," but generally there was no obvious comment.

Now let me be fair to the Harfats, the gnarled old boys. There was no racist baiting or chanting, nothing like that. It's just that the comedians in the crowd, once they've got their teeth into an offender on the opposing side, will tend to use any visual means at their disposal to have a go at him. There was a linesman, for example, with big ears, protruding teeth and dewlaps. So, predictably, once he'd given his first bum decision, Affie Morgans (a sort of self-appointed chief wit) was at him: "Keep up with the game, you ugly bugger." Likewise, a bald head is always good for a hoot or two of derision.

And so it was with "Magic". Around the half-hour mark, he was a little late into a tackle, and legged over one of the Town boys. And then they started, with Affie Morgans in the van: "Come on, Sambo. Back on the bloody jam pot!" Yes, it was innocence of a kind, naivety really, but all the voices and faces of my West Indian and West African friends were there in my mind, fidgeting uneasily.

With half-time came the official censure. The club chairman plodded over to the stand and gazed in with his long lugubrious face. "There's been a complaint from the visiting management, boys. Racial remarks about the darkie." He looked on gloomily, with an expression of sad rebuke, while Affie and the boys shuffled about and muttered things like, "Bit of fun, Dai, that's all." And, to be fair, there was no more barracking in the second half.

So what do I say? They're prejudiced, yes, but it's not neo-Nazi stuff. It *is* an innocence of a kind, and in some ways I can feel a wistful pull towards a little, out-of-the-way market town which hasn't really heard of things like apartheid, and where a black skin is like a bald head or protruding ears — a bit of ammo for the next intemperate bellow. As I say, these old boys aren't really prejudiced — just bloody gormless.

And, of course, I'll keep turning up to watch the team (and sit in the stand with the hecklers). It *is* a good side which, as I say, just needs a good goalscorer to round it off. I'll keep you posted.

Love to Gweno. Tell her Mrs. Beynon's cooking is all right, but it can't compete with hers.

Regards
Steve

*

c/o Beynon,
12 Rossetti Avenue,
Haverfordwest
23rd February 1991

Dear Watkyn,

I must have been sidetracked by other matters in recent letters, because I don't think I ever brought you up to date on the story of "Magic" and the local football team. The latest saga has been running for months now, since soon after I wrote to you about it first (in November-ish, I think).

Quite simply, I mentioned that the club were looking for a good goalscorer. Well, they signed one. "The experienced Arthur Roberts," said the local paper. We gathered he had been scoring freely for Margam. And the next Saturday out he ran: "Magic", no less. In a blur, we'd kicked off, and Magic's lithe brown figure was darting and probing at the head of our attack, while Affie Morgans and the other comedians sat gobsmacked in the stand.

Then, after a while, they seemed to warm to him slightly — after all, he clearly is a fine player. For a while, it was like a little gem of shy approval winking from the raucousness. "Come on, the coloured boy," said someone, and the stand all clapped polite-ly as Magic dummied a couple of defenders. Then, "Nice one, son." Generally, once a player is being called "son", he's halfway there. And by half time, as Magic showed some nice deft touches, he was gaining.

As I said, what we've needed is someone who could put the goals away. And early in the second half, Magic did just that. A ball bounced loose in the box and he clubbed it in with a super swinging volley. He was made. "Let's have you, Magic," they shouted. It was, as I remember, the only goal of the game, and there was even a ripple of applause as Magic left the field.

For perhaps five games, home and away, he couldn't go wrong. He got a goal or two every time. It was Magic, Magic, all the way. As games started, they'd be shouting to him, "Let's have you, Magic." Even, "Let's have a special, Magic." That's great, I thought. The barriers are down.

And then Magic went about four games without scoring. It happens to every striker, as you know. The team were back in their old ways: playing the football, creating the chances, and dropping points because they weren't putting the goals away. And late on, one muddy and frustrating afternoon, as Magic over-ran a pass, I heard Affie Morgans' grouchy comment, "Get hold of it, Sambo, for Christ's sake." And for a game or two then, it was back. A sort of weary grumbling: Sambo, darkie. What made matters worse was a really awful note by the club chairman in last week's programme, a silly set-up job, thanking the fans for their loyal support of the club and all its players, "regardless of racial origin".

In a purely footballing sense, I hope Magic stays. He's a super player and the goals are bound to come again. But what really gets to me, Watkyn, is the awful clumsy silliness of it all. As I say, it's a nice, easy, homely little town, and they're good old boys, most of them — but I do wish they'd come with us into the twentieth century.

Wearily then: all the best
Steve

*

c/o Beynon,
12 Rossetti Avenue,
Haverfordwest
17th March 1991

Dear Watkyn,

I'm writing sooner than planned because there is amazing news on the Magic front — stemming from a game yesterday.

I say "a game" — it was a local derby, the big one. The Town versus Pembroke Boro. To get the flavour of all this you need to know that, although the Boro have a hard core of two or three Swansea Jacks, most of them are local boys: hoofing great farming types from little villages down in the South of the county. And their supporters, as befits the denizens of a dockyard town, are *really* raucous — nearly in the Ton and Ferndale valleys class.

Some of their players, egged on by their fans, started niggling at Magic from the start. And you did get then (from the Boro fans) real needle: "darkie", "coon", you name it. And amazingly, our boys seemed to get a strange sort of injection of the protective impulse. "Sambo" was gone yesterday; it was all "Hang in there, Magic. You show him;" "Show them the way to goal, Magic." Even exhortations to violence: "Go on, Magic. Hang one on the bugger."

Once or twice, Magic showed real flashes of his class. The boys were getting behind him now, and he seemed to be thriving on it. Then, early in the second half, with the game deadlocked, no score, he cut loose. Two goals in about five minutes, and each one a beauty. Affie Morgans and all the gnarled old boys were roaring support and the Boro fans were beaten into a gloomy silence. Once again, it really was Magic, Magic, all the way. "Great game, Magic." He was applauded loudly all the way up the steps.

So, Watkyn. I'm asking you. Is this a triumph of quality over bigotry? Will Magic knock the barriers down in time? Or do you, like me, find it sad that he really does need a goal a game to get a decent crack of the whip?

I'll leave you with a postscript to all of this. I overheard Affie Morgans, rolling his corpulent bulk complacently off to the bar as the final whistle went, just saying to a mate, "If he can keep on getting goals like that, boy, he can be as black as he bloody likes."

Think on these things, Watkyn. I'm frankly perplexed.

Love to Gweno — and to yourself

Steve

POSTGIRL

O'Shaughnessy is intrigued, fascinated even (excited, let it be said), to look out of the front window of his cottage and to see a postgirl bringing mail to his door. She looks quite young, in her twenties say, with close-cropped, very dark hair (offset half-comically by the peaked cap perched upon it). She has large, luminous, very brown eyes, a full mouth and the trace of a snub nose, which makes her look almost like a schoolgirl — a schoolboy even. And grizzled, embattled 42-year-old O'Shaughnessy, surviving alone in his Camrose cottage, three miles out of town, is refreshed and pleased, watching the postgirl as she returns to her van and drives off.

O'Shaughnessy has always, until now, had his mail delivered by postmen (Colin and Jack, alternate weeks) but has gathered from a friend that they employ a few postwomen now. It is a concept he likes, that of the postgirl, for it fuses two of the things that move him most deeply: females and the post. Despite his two very unsuccessful marriages and several girl friends who all finally wrote him off as a feckless and irresponsible dreamer, O'Shaughnessy loves women. Likewise, in a very deep way, he is fascinated by the post. He is a writer, and although it is by his cluster of teaching and tutoring engagements that he pays the bills, it is in his poems and his stories that he most truly lives, and fuels his ambition. He once commented to a friend that practically every decision that really moved and excited him came to him through the post. Since he finds his small and undemanding garden a good place to potter in on spring, summer and autumn mornings, he can usually, on those days on which he is not teaching, break off from his writing about the time the post van comes round, and be out in the garden to collect the post and to chat to the postman.

*

Surely enough then, O'Shaughnessy is out in the garden when the new postgirl comes round next day. "Hello," she says, and "Hello. Thanks very much" says O'Shaughnessy, and they smile.

Things go on thus for a week (and then there's the alternate week, when Colin is coming round). The next week she addresses him by name. "Packet from Cardiff and a postcard, Mr. O'Shaughnessy."

Then, blurring his two enthusiasms into one, comes the morning of the decision he's been awaiting, from the magazine in South Africa, and their first real conversation.

"Airmail, Mr. O'Shaughnessy. South Africa."

He must look excited. "Good news?" she asks, looking amused.

"I'll tell you now," says O'Shaughnessy, opening the envelope. Ponders. Frowns. "Good-ish. It's what we call a friendly rejection. It's personalised. Do you see?" He shows her the rejection slip. "I sent a short story to a magazine in South Africa. I write quite a lot, you see."

"I know," she says. "I've read about you in the *Argus*."

"Well that, I'm sorry to say, is what we call a rejection slip. So just for the moment I'm disappointed. But the editor scribbled this note on it" — and he shows it to her again: "Although this one is not for us — perhaps the conclusion is a shade didactic — I did like the way you sustain an unusual narrative voice. Please do not hesitate to send us more of your fiction."

"So." O'Shaughnessy shrugs. "I'll let that sink in, and by lunchtime I'll be feeling quite good about it."

The girl looks curious. "So what will you do? Will you send them another story?"

"Oh, Lord, yes. That's quite enough encouragement."

"And how long will it all take?"

"South Africa, airmail, two ways. That's perhaps a fortnight. Also they've been a month deciding on this one. So: about six weeks in total."

"Right," says the postgirl. "I'll keep an eye out. Best of luck. Bye now."

*

A fortnight later, the letter from the BBC arrives, and it prompts O'Shaughnessy to invite the postgirl into his kitchen.

"BBC," she says, at the gate, looking quite intrigued. "I hope it's not another... what was it? ...rejection?"

"Let's take a look," says O'Shaughnessy. "Do you want to come in? Have a glass of squash or something?"

"Thanks," she says. "Yes."

In O'Shaughnessy's kitchen, he shows her the letter from the BBC. The producer of *Morning Story* doesn't in fact have a decision yet, and will let him know in about a fortnight. Meanwhile, they'll be repeating the *Poetry from Wales* series, which includes a couple of O'Shaughnessy's poems, so he should get a small cheque soon from the royalties department.

"That's great," says the girl. "You must be pleased." She hesitates for a moment. "Is it fun being a writer? Sorry. I don't mean 'fun'. Well… is it good?"

"Rewarding?"

"Yes. Rewarding. It must be."

"It's all I've ever really wanted to do. It can be lonely, so I'm glad I do quite a lot of teaching as well, so I can get out and meet people. But no, the writing is rewarding. And disappointing,when you get rejection slips."

"I didn't realise you taught as well."

"I have to. There's very little money in writing."

She nods. "So do you teach in a school?"

"Not often. It's mainly evening classes for adults. And a few afternoons down at the College."

She smiles. "That's interesting," she says. "I've never met a writer before, not a real one. Hey. I'd better get on. See you."

*

A fortnight later, the second BBC letter arrives and O'Shaughnessy learns that his *Morning Story* has been accepted. He and Jody (for the girl's name is Jody) celebrate in the kitchen with a glass of cider.

*

Now it is June, and Jody calls in for a glass of squash on two or three mornings a week. O'Shaughnessy was in fact told once by a friend that a few of the country postmen have their occasional watering holes, so he doesn't feel any qualms. And of course he likes her company. They usually scrutinise his mail and she is right up to date now with all his manuscripts and their progress. And they talk of many things. Nothing theoretical, they don't talk of politics or crime or education; they talk of bright and concrete things.

"Do you go shopping much?" he asks her one morning.

"Shopping?" says Jody. "Not much. But I don't know. I do a little, I suppose. I have a bit of a splurge about once a month, with some friends. Women are supposed to shop, aren't they? What about you?"

"Virtually never," says O'Shaughnessy. "I once bought the most awful Indian shirt, a Hare Krishna thing, in the hippy shop in Carmarthen, and I haven't been shopping since."

"I bet you go to bookshops."

"Bookshops, yes," he says. "I love bookshops. I browse and buy. And I also buy masses of postcards."

"Postcards? Do you collect them?"

"No, I use them. I send a lot of short notes and replies to people, and I like to have unusual postcards to send them on. I've generally got two or three dozen on hand at any time. Shall I show you what I've got now?" (My God, thinks O'Shaughnessy. This is Come-and-see-my-etchings stuff. But Jody is smiling happily and seems to see no irony.)

He shows her the postcards. Pubs in Powys, Series 2. The Old Oak in Carmarthen. The Augustus John portrait of Dylan. A couple of Knapp-Fisher reproductions. A few freaked-out Arthurian ones from a trip to Glastonbury. Two Degas, one Monet. Stained glass in Kings' College Chapel.

Jody is delighted. "I'll ask one favour," she says, "and then I'll go."

"The favour is…?"

"Send me one of your postcards for my birthday. August the seventh. I'll leave my address tomorrow. Okay? See you."

*

Doubts now creep into O'Shaughnessy's mind. Both his wives and all his girlfriends always said he was too self-centred, talking only of himself, uninterested in others. Jody has been calling for a couple of months now, and they talk of him, his writing. What of her? O'Shaughnessy thinks of *Othello:*

"She loved me for the dangers I had passed,
And I loved her that she did pity them".

"Have you ever read *Othello?*" he asks her next morning. "Or much Shakespeare?"

"*Antony and Cleopatra,*" says Jody, "and *Twelfth Night.* I did 'A' level English once, believe it or not. I passed it. And History. I could have gone to college, but I just couldn't get motivated. I thought I'd stay in town and work here — I like it in the Post Office — and I thought I'd maybe read. Only I don't. I read a lot, but mainly pulp fiction. I'm a slob." She grins. "I should read something of yours, shouldn't I? Where could I get your book?"

"There are copies in the library, and the Quay Street bookshop. But come on. Tell me about you."

"Wow," says Jody. "There isn't much to tell. Hobbies: jogging and aerobics. I jog in the weeks I'm out on the van. When I'm doing my town round, and walking, I reckon that's enough. And that's about it. I said: I'm a slob."

"You'd better get going then. Don't forget to call tomorrow… slob."

*

The next week, she is carrying a copy she's bought of one of O'Shaughnessy's two short story collections, and wants it autographed. He is about to write, "To Jody, the postgirl," then he checks himself. That is patronising, he thinks to himself. That is male vanity — arrogance of a kind. That's why half your other relationships broke up. He writes, "To Jody, with love. Tony O'Shaughnessy."

"That's great," she says. "I've never had a book autographed before. Hey, I'm thrilled. I've read the first two stories, and liked them. I'll read the rest on Sunday. Must go. See you."

She drains the rest of her squash, blushing slightly. She really does look pleased.

*

It is late July.

"Jody? Your birthday? August the seventh?"

"Yep. I wasn't going to tell you, but I'm twenty-three."

"Well..." He hesitates. "Okay. I hope this won't strike you as threatening, and obviously you'll have family commitments... Well. On your birthday, or when you like really — could I take you out to dinner?"

As she replies, slowly — and she seems confused and is blushing — it is as if waves of surf are pounding O'Shaughnessy's head.

"I don't know if I've ever been out to what you'd call dinner," she says. "I go out for meals. Like, dinner, as in...? Where would we go?"

"There's a few nice places," he says. "I don't go out much myself. I just thought..."

He knows and she seems to know this isn't working.

"I don't know," she says. "I mean... thanks so much, it's a really nice thought... Well, partly, I'm not sure what my boyfriend would think. I'm not that bothered what he thinks, really, but..." She looks very unhappy now, almost tearful. "Can I let you know?"

He nods.

"I'll let you know soon. And... oh... the other thing. This is a pity, and I was going to tell you... My rounds are changing from the start of August, and I've got two town rounds. No van. I won't be out here again after tomorrow."

*

My God, thinks O'Shaughnessy, after she's gone. My God. How utterly, unbelievably crass. Of *course* she's got a boyfriend, you stupid man. She might even live with him. She likes you, she likes the chat, but... God, you are so stupid. You've loused it all up again.

O'Shaughnessy's dreams seem to crumple in on him, like a pack of cards.

*

He does of course send her a postcard for her birthday. The Augustus John portrait of Dylan.

*

It is August now, and O'Shaughnessy still potters in the garden, picking up the mail from Colin and Jack. The South African magazine *does* accept his story, but the reply has come a lot more slowly than he'd expected. Obviously he's pleased, for he almost lives by and loves acceptances. And of course there's a twinge: he would so have loved Jody to have brought the letter and to have drunk a glass of cider with him to celebrate.

Then Colin brings one morning a single letter, local postmark, one he can't identify. Firm handwriting, probably female. He studies it in his kitchen, before opening it. It reads,

"Hi, it's me — Jody. How are you? This is just a sort of how-are-you-keeping letter and to say the town rounds aren't too bad, but I haven't got anyone nice I can call on. You can't on the town rounds anyway — you'd be spotted.

"Not much other news, except that I've split up with my boyfriend. I'd been going to for a while, I think. He was just too heavy and interfering. He was bad news. He did *literally* wear a medallion." (Then, crossed out, there was the phrase, "So that means..." The letter continued:) "There's not much other news, but do write back and tell me of anything new you're writing.

"I'm not being pushy, I hope, but if you *would* like that dinner some time, that's fine by me. Only I'll pay half. Postwomen don't earn much, but neither do writers, I don't suppose.

"Lots of love, Jody.

"P.S. Did you ever hear from that magazine in South Africa? J."

O'Shaughnessy pours himself a celebratory glass of cider. Then he has another. One is for South Africa, one is for Jody. And then he has a third, as Jody's celebration of South Africa. The fourth glass, to the boyfriend, he dedicates to "Absent Friends".

That afternoon, in the College, O'Shaughnessy delivers the most rollicking lecture on *Othello*.

*

It is September now, and O'Shaughnessy picks Jody up, from her parents' house, for their dinner at a country club near St. Davids. As they leave, her mother looks at O'Shaughnessy a little dubiously, but Jody trots out happily enough.

But, once they arrive at the restaurant, Jody seems to become nervous. When O'Shaughnessy says that he will pay, she seems too intimidated to argue. She is hopelessly overdressed, wearing something resembling a ball gown, which she says her mother made up five years ago before a Sixth Form dance at the local comprehensive school. O'Shaughnessy is wearing a pullover and open-necked shirt.

Something doesn't click, doesn't fall into place. They talk a little of manuscripts and writing, but they are going over old ground. Clumsily, he asks about aerobics and *her*, and she tells him a little. There's nobody else much in the restaurant to talk about, and she seems daunted by the presence of the waiter.

For months, they've chatted happily, for ten minutes at a time, before Jody has said, "Must go. See you." Now the full length of the evening has left them stranded. She is clearly unhappy and he is unhappy also. For the wine, the gentle lighting, all proclaim, "This is dinner. This is a relationship". They were both of them happier drinking squash in O'Shaughnessy's kitchen.

But, as he drops Jody off at her house, he kisses her good night (the first time he has kissed her, and possibly the last). She seems pleased to be kissed and kisses him back. Then she says, "The other thing. I didn't say this earlier, but our rounds are changing again soon. I think I'll be out your way again. Can I keep calling?"

"Of course you can. Thanks for your company."

"Thanks. Good night."

*

It's deepening into autumn now, and Jody is calling once again. Surprisingly, perhaps, they *do* pick up the threads. They are constrained for a while, naturally, there is a sense of embarrassment, but soon they are talking as before, of new submissions and of O'Shaughnessy's garden and, once, of Jody's new jogging circuit. For Christmas, he plans to send her another postcard, perhaps a

Monet. In an odd way, their friendship may even have mellowed a little. They treat each other very warily perhaps, but are very gentle with each other.

It won't last, of course; O'Shaughnessy realises that. Her rounds will change, and anyway, there will in time be other boyfriends,with or without medallions. But he and Jody are friends, she's a lovely girl and it's all a lovely interlude. Which is something. For such has been, very much, the story of O'Shaughnessy's life.

THE ROAD BACK

ONE: ALISON

God. Seven a.m. I heard the outside door closing, just a few minutes ago, so Stephen's gone, off on his trip to Wales. And, God, that is a big relief because for these last few days he has just been too, too nice. Courteous, charming — this morning he even brought me a cup of tea in bed. At half-past six, for God's sake. When you're getting over an affair — and that last one, that Marco, he was bad news, he just turned bloody nasty — the last thing you want is a ducky husband fussing over you.

And yet... I wonder. Is that really true? Is that really fair on me or on Stephen? Isn't that all a silly parody in a way? I mean, Stephen isn't that much of a dope. "Hello, dear, I'm glad your affair is over. Have a nice cup of tea." No, it's never quite that simple. I mean, does he know, first of all, about my affairs and my boy friends? Hell, he must do, he must realise, I must change, I get uptight and there's a nasty atmosphere here and he and the boys are down and restless. Then the affair blows over (maybe I see sense, for God's sake) and I feel very subdued and maybe even penitent. Perhaps that's what he and the boys feel, the change of mood, and he gets kinder again, and the boys are more themselves. I know that protective, fussy way of Stephen's is a pain in the bum on times — that's why I have my flings, I think — but sometimes, just sometimes, after one of my lovers has bashed his way out of my life, it's quite nice to have a devoted husband — or at least, one who seems and acts devoted. Maybe all my lovers are too brutal, like Marco, but however it is, and why ever it is, Stephen's quite a comfort after one of my flings.

And of course, this time it's all got mixed up with one of his trips to Wales. Once Stephen knows he's going down to Wales for a few days, he becomes very dreamy and kind, in a remote sort of way. He looks forward to it. And then of course I wonder: has he got a woman down there? Possibly not, possibly it's all legit, because his magazine has him down as "Welsh affairs correspondent". Although that is silly. I mean, that is so puerile. What sort of mag is that, that would bill the same guy as biological editor and Welsh affairs correspondent? We are talking now of a tatty little academic weekly and, on what Stephen brings home, we're talking of a tatty little academic salary. Come on, this flat, this bedroom, the comfort, they're down to me. I've worked my way up from researcher to presenter. I'm your media front-woman, your high-powered female, and I'm a big earner, so maybe, just maybe, if Stephen's clinging on to my coat tails and can afford to take a job with a crappy little environmentalists' mag, then maybe I deserve a fling and a lover from time to time.

But Wales. Our Welsh affairs correspondent. Yes, I'm sure it is legit, I've seen his features. This time he's doing... what?... that oil tanker spillage in Pembrokeshire a few months back. But yes, he does seem so faraway and dreamy before going off, and I do wonder if he's got a woman there. I don't suppose I've any right to be jealous, but I am.

And then again, maybe he hasn't. Stephen and this Wales business are impossible, but then quite a few Welsh people in London have this silly Garden-of-Eden thing in their heads. I mean, Stephen grew up on the Dale peninsula, for Christ's sake, and I've only been down there with him a few times, but that little place was just about falling off the end of the earth. And then, Jesus, his agricultural college. How many TV presenters have got husbands who went to agricultural college? I know he jacked it all in, he was doing his biology degree when I met him, but I reckon that if Stephen had had a family farm to go to, he'd have been there like a shot. I mean, that college he went to, the one with the margarine advert name. Golden Grove! That is just over the top, that is the Eden myth. And he does still hanker after it. He gets the *Carmarthen Journal* sent on every week, for God's sake, and browses round the news of the farms and the marts.

In a way, Stephen and I get on well enough — or well enough until that damn placid, easy nature of his drives me to another fling. I think it is the easygoing manner which irritates me, the innocence. Because, God, when we first met and I seduced him, he was so innocent. It was so manifestly and so embarrassingly his first time. It was weird. I stroked his member and it did arouse him, certainly, but he seemed to be waiting, gazing at the damn thing as if fascinated, anyone would have thought he'd never had an erection before. In the end, he only just got it in in time. Which, of course, is not much fun for the female party.

I must admit though that he got it in to pretty good effect, because Robin was conceived. Indeed, the other two followed with three years, so there's not too much wrong with Stephen in the sperm department. I suppose really there's nothing totally wrong with him in bed, now he's used to it. He's what you'd call a good journeyman, I suppose. An honest workmanlike performer. No frills, no novelties, just good straight sex. Which isn't always enough, I'd reckon — and hence Marco and my other flings. But how many? Hell. Four of them, really. In sixteen years of marriage. And anyway, I've had enough of flings for now so maybe, when Stephen gets back, we'll settle for a while to a domestic respectable rhythm and domestic respectable sex. For that is Stephen, he's respectable, he's proper, very proper. He took a little seducing, but he absolutely had to do the right thing then, and marry me. And I thought, well, he's kind, he's agreeable, as well him as another. I couldn't have coped with the Marco type for a husband. So maybe I am better off with domestic Stephen bringing me a cup of tea in bed, and then him drifting off to Wales from time to time. I suppose he's what you'd call, in quotes, a good husband. Boring on times, but a good husband. And the boys like him. They think he's a great guy, they like the placidity and the properness even, and they talk to him. More than they do to me, in fact. Maybe I'm jealous about that as well...

TWO: STEPHEN

Stephen's car edged out of London and on to the motorway. For a long while, he brooded quietly, finding very little in the drive to interest him. He would soon be passing through some farming country, in Berkshire and Wiltshire, and it was early summer, so there should have been some interest in that, but the real buzz wouldn't come for him until he'd crossed the Bridge into Wales and set off up the Wye Valley to connect with the road he wanted, the road that would lead him through the sheep farms along the River Usk and the Brecon Beacons, the road that would lead him eventually to the Towy Valley, and Bethan. That then would be farming country and it would be Wales, and that, for Stephen, would be a deep pull.

For the moment, however, on the motorway, the places he passed, Reading and Newbury, and in time there'd be Swindon, were just names written largely on great destination signs. Since Wales (and even Bethan) did not loom too largely in his thoughts just for the moment, his mind drifted back to Alison and the last few days.

For a long time, Stephen had assumed that Alison's jarring and unpleasant moods of brittle gaiety (lasting for weeks, or months even) were connected with affairs she might be having from time to time.He wondered sometimes if he might (or even should) be more resentful and jealous. He was bitter, in a way, of course he was, but the feature of his life in London which brought him most solace was his very comfortable and happy bond with his three teenage sons. In no way would he ever be without them or would he risk the kind of separation that a marriage breakdown would bring. At some point, in the future, when the boys had gone, then maybe. But in any case Stephen's was a placid nature and one which valued social propriety very highly. He found the idea of divorce and separation distasteful.

Nonetheless, he hated the false brilliance which glistened off Alison when, as he supposed, her affairs were going on. Afterwards, she'd seem to soften, she'd be humbled and some-times hurt (for which he felt no particular sympathy), but it did at least mean that they could slip into a more or less agreeable kind of mutually accepting domesticity. Alison was an intelligent con-versationalist and, if they stayed on neutral topics, they could pot-ter on agreeably enough for a year or so — or years sometimes. As the glib media phrase has it, they gave each other space. And all of that — the placidity, the calm between the threatening storms — he wanted for his boys.

All this seemed ill-thought-out and Stephen was conscious, as he neared the Bridge, that he'd thought very little through that morning. But the movement of his car in a few short miles — over the Bridge, off the motorway, into Wales and on to the side road up the Wye Valley — this transition was a sea-change, something he always regarded as almost symbolic, of homecoming, Bethan, everything. His final destination on this trip was in fact Pembrokeshire, but he'd be stopping and staying first in the Towy Valley, that fertile region which he'd thought of now, for twenty years, as a kind of home.

He'd gone there first from school, and had spent two years in the agricultural college in Golden Grove. Only later, realising that without a family farm to inherit, he wasn't going to get far in farming, did he make the gradual journey East: to a biology degree in Cardiff, and then, after the rushed marriage to Alison, to London as the husband backing up her glamourous television career, himself taking a succession of jobs with a variety of environmental organisations and magazines. The jobs were all right; he quite enjoyed his work.

Farming of course might have been so different. As he passed the sheep farms above the River Usk and knew in himself that, as the journey unwound, there were dairy farms (and one in particular) to come, Stephen began to feel a deep sense of peace. The very sight of a farmhouse, nestling among the green, its tractors, its dogs, its outbuildings — all of this could bring him sometimes almost a moment's epiphany, something blessed, something magical. In a very soothing and curious way, he felt and thought of farmhouses as feminine. During his one summer vacation at Golden Grove, hoping to pick up experience which might get him into the farming world, he'd taken a job as farmhand with a man called Morgan, who ran a dairy farm in the Towy Valley. So much about that summer captivated him, but a deep and abiding memory was that of the family's females, at their butter - and whey-making...

*

"My memories of that summer, 1976, are quite magical and are dominated in my memory's texture, by sights and sounds and smells. Smells in particular, I think, notably the deep scent of newly-mown hay, warm and omnipresent. There were other smells too, like those of thyme and mint, drifting off the farm and off the countryside, so that, in bed at night, I could feel the heat and scent of the evening as an almost tangible entity.

"There were so many sights as well, of the dairy in particular. The old crafts were still practised on most of the farms in the Towy Valley, particularly by the families' daughters, and so there was whey, dripping from cheese vessels into brass pans. There were great pots full of a quite golden cream. There were eggs in pans, white, brown, and the blue-white ducks' eggs. Butter stood printed in shallow tubs, ready, like most of the dairy produce, to be taken off on Saturdays to the market in Carmarthen.

"The Morgans had two sons in their twenties, and two daughters. Charlotte, the elder, was eighteen. She had fluffy brown hair, she was composed and she was pretty. I was just a year older than she, and I very rapidly went along with the idea that I should take her to dances in Carmarthen as my partner. She was sweet, she was calm, and, in a quite undramatic way, we were able to enact a kind of boy- and girl-friend role for the summer, conversing and dancing happily, cuddling just a little as the Land Rover was driven back from Carmarthen by some local chaperon.

"I even had a rival. Arwel Tomos was, in farming terms, the boy next door; he was twenty-one and his father owned the farm a quarter-of-a-mile up the valley. Arwel was a tall handsome boy, with rich jet-black hair, a broad smile and a ringing laugh. The Towy Valley wasn't quite, in the 1970s, in the age of arranged marriages, but I do think that the Morgans had maybe hoped that Arwel might marry one of their daughters. He'd been out with Charlotte intermittently over the previous year, but seemed to feel no real jealousy at my brief intervention, seeming to regard it rather as a harmless interlude, as did the Morgans. Indeed, there were occasions when the three of us went to the dance in Carmarthen together. On no side did passions run high.

"It was with Bethan, the younger daughter, that I felt the passion, mine for her most certainly, and, I was almost as sure, hers for me. She captivated me. Being younger, she lacked her sister's elegance, but had the sort of natural grace and composure which seems sometimes to be born of innocence. Her moods seemed to alternate between solemnity and playfulness. She was very dark, and so dainty that it always took me by surprise to see her deftly handling pans of whey and butter. Then, now and again, her solemnity would melt, and she'd smile at me, sweetly and capriciously. After a few weeks, if passing me in a passageway or in the dairy, she'd smile and even sometimes nestle up close to me.

"Her family noticed the smiles and seemed amused as much as anything. 'Our Bethan's taken a shine to you, boy. Now give Stephen a little peace, Bethan. He doesn't want you making those cow's eyes at him all evening.' Perhaps they saw her as the sort of playful child that kind of remark suggests, but I was deeply aware of her profound combination of composure, artlessness and, not quite disguised by her daintiness, a rich bodily maturity. Her very presence filled me with a sense of love and excitement.

"And, just as forcefully, I was horrified with myself with what I was doing — or feeling. For Bethan was only fifteen. I was fully four years older and that seemed to be then an insuperable barrier. The age of consent of sixteen lurked uneasily in my mind, even though I had no intention whatever of making love to her, or kissing her or cuddling or anything. I just felt that it was wrong actually to love her. Yet I did.

"One Saturday, so many men were taken up with the haymaking that there was no-one left to drive Bethan to Carmarthen market where she (and Charlotte sometimes) ran a dairy stall. She smiled at the family happily. 'Stephen will take me,' she said. 'He's come to learn about farming.'

"So I drove her and the dairy produce into the county town, to admire there the composure with which she dealt with so many customers, most of them seemingly regulars. It's the sounds I remember most about Carmarthen market: the rattle of the place, the haggling and bartering, the conversations in their easy West Walian lilts. Most of Bethan's conversations with her customers were in fact in Welsh, always very demure and polite, for she really had the most delightful manners and a very natural ability to charm. And, after such conversations, she'd turn and smile at me, giving me the gist of what had been said. The Morgans' first language was of course Welsh, but they'd always, out of a natural courtesy, switch to English in my presence.

"We packed away at six, contented after our busy, happy day. As we settled into the front seat of the Land Rover, ready to go home, Bethan said, 'Thank you for coming with me, Stephen. I loved having you with me.' And she leaned over and kissed me, gently but firmly, on the mouth.

"I was enraptured, startled (and even fearful) and could only blurt out, 'Bethan, you're only fifteen.' The look she gave me was unabashed, but calm and still oddly composed. 'I'll be older soon,' she said. 'I just wanted to show you I was grateful.' Nervously, uncertainly (but unable to gainsay a lurching mood of very deep delight) I started the engine and we set off back to the farm. We talked gently, along the way, of Bethan's customers in Carmarthen, and of the coming Young Farmers' Club dance.

*

The journey, from the banks of the Usk and across the Beacons, had been quicker than Stephen had expected. Now he had driven through Llandovery (stopping briefly at the florist's) and, in Llandeilo, had turned off on to the Golden Grove road and into the Towy Valley. He drove straight to the village and parked by the churchyard. He let himself in by the lych-gate, went across and, very tenderly, laid his flowers on Bethan's grave.

*

"Bethan wasn't allowed to go to the dances and discos in Carmarthen with me and Charlotte, but her parents made an exception in the case of the Young Farmers' Club dance, which many younger children attended. She'd been clearly looking forward to it for days, smiling and winking at me occasionally and saying, with an odd kind of innocent bravado, that she'd dance with me all night if I gave her the chance. 'Bethan, you're shocking,' said her mother. 'Give the poor boy a rest.' Still the Morgans seemed to look on her as an artless child; perhaps she was artless, but I began to suspect that she felt as deeply for me as I did for her — and that she would be artless enough to be very open about her affection.

"The dance was homely and breezy, very much in the Young Farmers' tradition. There was relatively little smooching and, better, little of the grim solemnity I'd associated with the discos I'd been to. This in fact was a genuine old-fashioned dance. There was some real country dancing, and there was also a sequence, through the evening, of waltzes, foxtrots and quicksteps, the kind of dance which had elsewhere (even in Pembrokeshire) long gone out of fashion.

"One distinctive aspect of the waltz and the foxtrot, of course, is the physical closeness between yourself and your partner. I danced with Charlotte and many others, aware of contact then maybe, but when I came to dance with Bethan (as I did frequently, because she came to ask me at every Ladies' Choice and Excuse Me) I was more than aware of our closeness — I was near to ecstasy at times, and, uneasily mixed, elation and worry, as our breaths mingled and our thighs and breasts nudged gently together. She managed to partner me again for the Last Waltz and, as the

46

lights faded, kissed me again, first on the cheek and then on the lips. I was quite aware now of being in love with her — utterly captivated by her ingenuous flattery, delighted by her pursuit of me. And, at the same time, her youth and the difference in our ages nagged horribly in my mind, as if I were close to some very dreadful wrong.

"Three nights later, she met me leaving the dairy quite late in the evening, when everyone else was back in the farmhouse. 'Shall we go for a walk?'" she said, and took my hand. By now, all my will had gone.We made our way to the hayloft and snuggled away, away from everyone, in the warmth and hay-scent and half-light. We partially undressed, removing trousers, jeans and underwear.

"And then suddenly, the moment stilled and the mood changed. I'd had very little experience with girls, but only now did I realise that Bethan must have had very little to do with boys. Everything slowed down and, I think, in retrospect, it is that which gave the moment its extraordinary beauty. Still that voice in my head said, You can't, she's only fifteen — and because of that I made no move to make love to her. We sat, fascinated by each other, filled with wonderment at the sight and proximity of each other's nakedness — a wonderment at this new strange loveliness which had come upon both of us.

"Much of the composure had gone from Bethan now. She looked both happy and bewildered — as I was myself. Slowly, shyly now, and rather gauchely, she reached out and fumbled wonderingly with my penis. And then, with a gasp and a rush, my semen spilled and splashed out, over her thighs and mine. A globule nestled in the little tuft of her pubic hair. I was close to weeping, from frustration and delight, and, for what seemed a long time, we clung together, whispering endearments. Only in time did we recover, and she asked, 'Didn't you want to? Have the whole thing?'

"'Bethan, we mustn't. You're still only fifteen."

"She looked at me very sadly. 'You will keep coming here to see me?'

"'Of course.'

"We dressed,and walked slowly back to the farmhouse."

*

47

In the mild early summer sunshine, Stephen gazed at the headstone, the familiar tears prickling behind his eyes. The headstone was inscribed in Welsh, of course, but Stephen knew that it commemorated the life of Bethan Tomos, who died on 12th April, 1984, aged 23 years. A devoted wife to Arwel, and mother to Mair and Hannah.

He would walk around the churchyard for a while now, look a last time at the headstone and his flowers and prepare for his visit to the farmhouse. Just as the prickling of his initial tears had been predictable, so increasingly, with every visit now, he began to be suffused with a growing sense of acceptance and even serenity. Bethan and his memories of her were becoming increasingly a reassurance.

He'd now drive to the farm, to visit Charlotte, who still lived, unmarried and with her parents. She, her parents and brothers were always welcoming; he was now an old friend of the family. They'd talk of the farm and the valley, the markets, of his job with the magazine, what his sons were doing. It would be unlikely that anyone would mention Bethan, but Stephen felt strong enough about her now to talk and think about her on occasions as when, about two years earlier, he had had the breathtaking experience of meeting Bethan's younger daughter Hannah. Indeed, he had been more delighted than distressed at the little girl's playfulness, with all the emotional echoes it created.

He'd wondered so often why he'd never really been able to resume the relationship with Bethan after the happiness of the '76 summer. He'd gone back, to visit the farm, during his second year at Golden Grove and had met Bethan frequently, but always in the company of her family. She'd seemed a little tense on times, and then, quite often, the old warmth would bubble out into a happy smile. He'd been uncertain, desperately so. On times, he'd reflected uncomfortably on the strict and censorious sense in which their evening in the hayloft had been an offence against the law, although that particular feeling eased very largely as the years went by.

After he'd left Golden Grove, and started his degree course in Cardiff, he'd still go back to the Morgans' farm, still awkward, still uncertain, very much aware that neither he nor Bethan really knew now how to resume their friendship. He'd given her the address of his flat in Roath and invited her (and Charlotte — for Stephen had still had the same streak of propriety) to call on him when, as occasionally, they'd get a train from Carmarthen to Cardiff and go shopping for the day. But they'd never called.

His last meeting with Bethan had been during his third year in Cardiff. As he recalled now, so sadly, he'd have been twenty-two and she eighteen. He'd called unexpectedly, being headed for Pembrokeshire. The talk in the family was all of the coming party to celebrate Bethan's engagement to Arwel Tomos. Bethan and Stephen communicated very little that evening, and he came away distraught. Just over a year later, he married Alison. He was jealous of Arwel, bitterly so (despite knowing the kindness and warmth of the man), and jealous in a way he never had been of Alison's supposed lovers. He did send a wedding present, because he'd wanted to for Bethan's sake, but it had hurt him badly.

Thereafter, curiously, it was Charlotte with whom he very occasionally corresponded; she wrote to tell him of the births of Bethan's daughters. He'd known nothing of Bethan's cancer, but Charlotte had written, just after the funeral, to tell him of her death; in fact, he'd read her obituary the day before in the *Carmarthen Journal*.

The five years between Bethan's engagement and her death had been an awful limbo, made bearable only because it was so mercifully peopled by the births and infancies of his sons. Her death had hurt him profoundly and, for over a year, he had stayed away, until eventually the lure of the valley had drawn him back one spring morning to lay flowers on Bethan's grave. He had haltingly kept re-visiting the churchyard and had soon felt the strength and the wish to re-visit the farm. The sense of solace grew. He rarely mentioned Bethan when he went to the farm, but, when he was there (and he felt, with such a sense of comfort, that he wanted to be there) the recollections and the reminders were all around — in the yard, in the farmhouse, in the dairy.

For many, many years now, his fondest and deepest thoughts (increasingly now, many of his happiest thoughts) had always been with Bethan and the Towy Valley.

THREE: CHARLOTTE

It's lovely and warm tonight, a real summer evening. The smells of mint and thyme are floating in through my bedroom window. It's on times like this that I'm glad I live and work on a farm.

And it was lovely to see Stephen today. It's nice to think a successful man like that will remember old friends. He's a writer with a London magazine and his wife's on television, and yet he always calls when he's back in Wales. We talked of all sorts of things, local things, and he told us about his family. He is so proud of his sons, it's always nice to see that. And he wanted to know how we were doing, he always does.

And... yes... I'm bound to wonder this. He never mentioned Bethan at all. Often he doesn't. I'll go down tomorrow and see if he's put flowers on her grave again.

Bethan was very fond of Stephen, I do know that. I remember the summer he stayed with us. She was only fifteen then and I felt, at the time, she might be getting in a little deep. I do remember glimpsing her kissing him after the Last Waltz at the Young Farmers' dance. Even the next year, and she was only sixteen then, she used to get very excited, agitated really, before he called, and I always wondered if she was, maybe, a little young. Maybe, I felt, if they took time and he could still call and they could get to know each other... well, maybe. Stephen's a nice person, and I think, I think, he was very fond of her. And yet, when he came here, the next year and the year after, he seemed very awkward and unsure of himself. I know he was a very correct sort of person and I know he'd never have taken advantage of Bethan or anything like that, but I didn't want her getting too involved and getting hurt. The next summer, he was in Cardiff then, and he gave us his address in Roath. Two or three times a year Bethan and I would take the train up to go shopping. And the first time we went, Bethan was edgy and odd and quiet for most of the day, and just said, when we were sitting in a tea-room, "Which way would we get to Roath, Charlotte?" And I said — and I think this was the right thing to have done, I've balanced it out so often in my mind — I said I wasn't sure. Maybe we'd call on him some other time. It was getting close to the time for our train. We'd see. Rather like a parent, really.

A few months later, when we were up again, Bethan asked again. "How would we get to Roath, Charlotte?" and really, my heart melted, I felt so sorry for her, for she did care for him, I knew she did. So we hunted and asked around the bus station and caught a bus to Roath. We found the flat (in an ugly old building) but there was nobody in. Bethan looked very down, so I suggested we cross over to the park, I could see there was a lake there, and walk around a little in the sunshine.

And then we saw Stephen, with a crowd of students — or I assume they were students. And they were wild. Coming from our background, from the farm, we were taken aback. They were playing music, on a transistor or a tape, playing it very loud, the Sex Pistols, I think. For they were real punks. There were quite a few of them with Mohican haircuts, and a couple had those safety pins in the nose. There was one man, or boy, lying with his head in a girl's lap. Both of them had Mohican cuts. Stephen was on the edge of the group, not so wild, he was just casually dressed, and he was with a girl. Just with her, really. I think he may have had his arm around her. I must say, and I must be fair, that he looked out of place among the punks. Who the girl was I've never known. It wasn't the woman he's married to, I know, for she's on television and she's blonde. This girl in Roath Park was dark. And just ordinary.

I'm still bound to wonder if we should have gone over to talk to him or even if that was what Bethan wanted. I didn't really feel I could cope with it, and I might have had to take the lead, for she looked very confused and unhappy. In the end, I just asked, "What shall we do, Bethan? Shall we go for our train?" And she nodded. On the way back she was very, very quiet, close to tears, I think. On the journey she just said, once, "I think Stephen's gone away from me now, don't you?" I had to reply I thought maybe he had.

For a while, Stephen called again on occasions, but they were both very quiet now, almost unhappy, it seemed. And then she got engaged to Arwel. Arwel had been very fond of her for years, obviously, and Bethan seemed to go over to him very quickly, after the business in Roath park. And she and Arwel were very happy together, I think.

After the engagement, Stephen stayed away for a long while. He and I wrote occasionally, and he'd send presents, for the wedding and when the girls were born. Bethan never told him (and I didn't feel I could tell him) about her cancer. He didn't come to the funeral, but he wrote to me a few days afterwards. His letter was very formal but very sweet, and I've kept it. And then, a year or so later, he started to call again. Now he is, yes, I suppose he's an old friend of the family. And a very loyal friend, a very kind one. And always there'll be flowers for Bethan's grave.

So I do wonder sometimes if I broke up a love affair. Or, no, that's not quite right — perhaps I stood by and watched it break up. I don't know. But Stephen has a fine life now, I'm sure. He's got three lovely sons, he's got a job writing with a London magazine, and he has that beautiful wife, who's on television so often. He wouldn't have been satisfied, not really satisfied, not for ever, with Bethan and the Towy Valley.

BETTY'S GIRL

Tracy had a presence that was warm and young and physical. That doesn't mean that she was any kind of tart. As she moved softly and daintily about the counter in the snack bar its customers were aware of a slightly tousled blonde, a slim leggy girl with plump neat buttocks whose breasts bobbled just a little as she moved across to wait at the tables. There was something perhaps mildly provocative in her occasional wearing of a pair of imitation leopardskin jeans with the motif "Hands Off" inscribed across one buttock, but even in that she seemed to project, in a way, a curious kind of innocence.

This innocence must have derived in part from Betty's protective presence alongside her in the cafe. Betty's snack bar had been open in the centre of town for around fifteen years and Betty, forty, fifty, fifty-five years old, brawny and formidable, had watched over a succession of young waitresses, always with the sense that they were her girls, Betty's girls, and that loose or offensive chat from customers was not expected. There may have been working for her over the years, a series of girls who were variously slim, buxom, leggy and attractive, but it was an understood attitude of the house that Betty's girls were reserved into a kind of mild inviolability which the patron had created for their protection.

This was perhaps particularly so in Tracy's case, for Tracy who had been working for Betty since leaving school a year earlier, was a relative, a daughter of Betty's cousin. They were both Donovans and there'd been several families of Donovans living for years in and around the Square, a large area of council housing on the edge of town. By this time Betty, whose snack bar was thriving and whose husband Des had a good job in the County Offices, had moved to an altogether grander house on a private estate a little further out, but as she passed through the Square on her way into town in the mornings she'd pick up her young relative from the corner.

Her protectiveness towards Tracy was in part a family thing: the Donovans had always been very close and Betty was anxious that her young cousin should be properly respected and treated. But it stemmed in part also from a particular view of men and women that was perhaps very basic to Betty's own personality. Betty's own husband Des was a very meek, kindly little man, a shade faded by now perhaps, shabby and droopily-moustached, but he and Betty had always had the kind of ploddingly successful marriage that allowed Betty the freedom to run her business, and had seen their own daughter safely through school, off to a catering diploma course, and on to a comfortable marriage and the running of a small family hotel in the West Country.

What Betty mistrusted in contrast to all this placidity was, if we're honest, glamour. Over the years several of her younger waitresses had been very open to the blandishments and chatting-up of the motley bunch of postmen, shop assistants, office workers and truck drivers who moved through the snack bar in an average day. Betty knew that men were ready to flirt and she mistrusted that a little; they were capable also of a crude and suggestive wit and this Betty hated. Romance (if that's what people called romance) had never figured too prominently in Betty's life (apart from one broken engagement before Des's time) and now, if any of her girls did start getting too openly fresh with male customers, it was a fair chance the girl would find the atmosphere getting stiff enough to persuade her to move on after a while. Indeed, there was a fair chance that the customer himself would be made to feel very uncomfortable before it was all over. Betty's view of men, romance and marriage was simple to the point of being primitive: you either found a quiet respectable man (like Des) and you settled into a married routine where you could speak your mind and be yourself — or you got ensnared by some he-man glamourboy and spent the rest of your days (as indeed had a few of Betty's friends and relatives living now in the Square or thereabout) regretting your mistake, as you were pushed into pegging out lines of washing, behind lines of kids, in the wake of some drunken bully.

Yes, of course it was simplified, and of course she was a social snob. She did, to be fair, keep up a strong loyalty to various friends, sisters and cousins still living in and around the Square, but she was glad that she herself had moved out to a private estate. Perhaps her snobbery showed as much in her differing views of the occupations of her male customers. In the mornings, the snack bar was a frequent haunt of shop assistants, occasional office workers and postmen who'd just finished their rounds and Betty regarded this group as respectable enough. The problem, as she saw it, would arise, often in the evenings, with long-distance lorry drivers who'd park in the riverside car park and call in for an evening meal before going off for bed and breakfast or before a drive home. Some of them certainly could be lecherous and suggestive, the chat in the snack bar at five and six o'clock could get more bawdy, and Betty hated it. For business' sake she had to tolerate it a little but she usually retaliated after a while. She'd developed most certainly by this time a very deep prejudice against truck drivers. (Indeed her own ex-fiancé had been a truck driver.)

And so, because of all of that, when Betty realised that Rancho had taken a fancy to Tracy and — worse — that Tracy was quite impressed by him, Betty was quite savagely irate. Rancho was a Cardiff boy around his mid-twenties, unmarried he claimed (but Betty was often reluctant to believe that particular story) and working for a firm of hauliers who sent him on twice-weekly runs to town.

In a way Betty's prejudices against him were justified. He really was the archetypal medallion man, through to the hairy chest and the loud-mouthed chat. And he said, suddenly, one evening, "Why you got 'Hands Off' across there, love? Hands off except for Rancho, is it?" And then, as Tracy trotted back to the counter, blushing a little hotly (but not too unhappily, it seemed) Rancho grinned around at his mates. "I likes to see them blushing, son. I likes a bit of spirit."

That was enough for Betty. For a couple of weeks she'd been watching Tracy take Rancho's meal across and noticed a genuine difference in the girl, for Tracy's manner in the cafe up till then had suggested, as much as anything, a kind of fluffy innocence. Now all Betty could see was a dreadful kind of pseudo-sultriness that she suspected the girl had picked up from magazine covers and television — all this designed doubtless to live up to Rancho's assumed expectations.

It was time now for Betty to intervene. She drove Tracy off to the Square that evening in a stony silence before just commenting curtly as she dropped the girl off, "I don't like that Rancho. He's a hard man — and he's mean. Just be careful with him, Trace."

Tracy looked a little nettled and tossed her head a trifle petulantly. "I quite like men to be hard, Bet. And anyway, he's not mean. He always buys a round of tea."

This short exchange seemed to annoy Tracy. Talking to her cousin Juliette about it the next weekend she grumbled freely and added, "Bet's probably just jealous."

Juliette, a single parent who was herself arguably the victim of a Rancho-style infatuation, was left to puzzle over that.

"She probably is jealous, Trace — in a way I mean — well, you know old Des. He can't exactly be a ball of fire at night-time. But there you go. She's safe and she's free. It's probably the best way for a woman."

This to Tracy was very negative but the line of thought ran on through Juliette's head long after Tracy had left. Yes, Betty was very rigid — either you got the better of a man or he got the better of you. And sure, romance was out for Betty. Nobody knew for certain what had happened with Betty's truck driver all those years ago but the family reckoned that Betty had been too aggressive for him. It was he who had broken it off apparently.

So Juliette was still left pondering. Left alone on the Square, with the two kids and every other man you met assuming you were an easy lay, she often reckoned she'd settle for a nice quiet husband. But would she settle for Des, she wondered? Trim dainty little Des, moustache and waistcoat, with his gloves and his purse — "damn nearly a handbag" one of the cousins had said once. Juliette was left wondering.

Betty meanwhile wasn't giving in. From the day of their exchange at the Square, she set out to keep Tracy out of Rancho's way. Betty would take his meal across now, despite Rancho's grumbles.

"Where's little Leopardskin then, Missus? I'll keep my hands off, honest." Curtly, Betty would address him always as 'Mister' and bang his plate down just a shade too noisily. After a while she'd forget the salt, slop his tea — always calculated insolence until in time Rancho had had enough and rose to an inevitable outburst, "Ah, sod you. Just give us the bill, you stupid old cow. And stuff your sodding snack bar." He barged out.

Very slowly Betty quietly mopped up the sugar she'd spilt onto Rancho's half-empty plate and took the plate back to the counter while Rancho's mates looked on, a little startled and embarrassed. But all Betty could think of was what Tracy was going to say. For this was the test clearly. And what she said came as a huge relief. Flushed and indignant she gazed at Betty and muttered, "The cheeky bugger. The stupid pillock. If he can talk to you like that, Bet, he can get stuffed as far as I'm concerned."

The summer which followed was a gentle easy one. Tracy seemed to thrive now and Betty basked in that assurance. As I said, the morning and early evening clienteles of the snack bar were slightly different so there seemed nothing untoward when Tracy suddenly seemed to develop a warm fondness for one of the morning postmen, a lad of much her own age, called Ronnie. Everything about Ronnie (even his job, of course) was right, as far as Betty was concerned. He and Tracy were going out regularly, Tracy would chatter to Bet happily in the car about the places they'd been, and she'd serve him, with a gently unostentatious flirtation in the snack bar. Even Tracy's manner had changed. She seemed to have lost the magazine-cover sultriness she'd affected for Rancho's benefit. The mood of her and Ronnie's fondness was a simple boy-and-girl one, which was fine. Tracy was after all only eighteen. She'd trot happily towards him with just a gently bobble of the breasts and the same ingenuousness she'd shown before Rancho had appeared.

Come autumn, Betty took a week off, left a cousin in charge, and she and Des went to Blackpool. And, as soon as she was back, as Tracy got into her car by the Square that Monday morning, Betty knew there was something wrong — a stiffness, a reserve. She noticed also that Tracy was wearing the "Hands Off" leopardskin jeans again; they'd disappeared all summer. When Ronnie didn't show up that morning and Tracy stayed aloof and distant, Betty was all the more concerned. Indeed by five o'clock when the new medallion man appeared, Betty was half expecting him.

His name was Hoppy, he was from Swansea, an ex-professional footballer he reckoned and he was driving with a firm that had a new contract with a construction company locally for the next six months. All this Betty gleaned from Tracy's own remarks and from loud comments passed across the cafe by Hoppy himself. Tracy herself took his meal over and Betty didn't find it worth her while to stop the girl. There again was the sultry pose, the turn of the head, the flash of the buttock. And there, as predictably, was Hoppy's response, "I likes to see that 'Hands Off' sign, love. Gives me something to aim for."

And Betty saw only too clearly, with a deep and painful sadness that had very little to do with jealousy, that there lay ahead for Tracy, not with Hoppy necessarily or Rancho, but with someone like them, a future that had been enacted already on the Square and on a thousand Squares — the bullying, the cramping and a slow sad subjugation. Betty may have been right and she may have been wrong but this is what she saw and what she felt and there was nothing, nothing, nothing she could do.

QUEEN OF THE CANDY STORE

It's a quite lovely morning, it's only quarter-to-seven, and you are looking out of your bedroom window at Castle Back. The town is beautiful: the houses, chimneys, gables, sheds, the tucked-away jumble of the middle of town. And you are beautiful too. It's just quarter-to-seven, and you don't have to be in the shop till nine. You have all that time to ease awake.

First you'll indulge yourself. There'll be time in plenty to wash and change, so first you'll walk about a while in the nude, in front of the mirror. You're lovely — and you know it and they know it, the town crowd, the punters, your many admirers. Be kind to yourself, there are few women of forty with nude bodies like yours to boast about. Your breasts are small but plump, and your buttocks are round and cupped, with not a trace of middle-aged spread. Aren't you the pretty one? And then you glimpse the triangle of pubic hair and you reflect that no-one but you has ever gazed upon it. Bomber, poor Bomber, he never glimpsed your privacy. It was dark, that night, and it was just the one time. It was his first time, like yours, he said so, and you were sure anyway.

That's probably why people feel sorry for you, but they needn't. Part of you always wanted to stay tucked away in town — and part of you is very happy to be as beautiful as you are. But there's the old argument, isn't there, Beauty versus Brains, and women wanting to fulfill themselves, so they feel sorry for you. To them, you're a victim. You were the good little grammar school girl, English, History and Scripture in the Sixth Form, and you went out for six months with a boy from the Naval base, and you got pregnant. Then his long leave, then he got posted, but you're not blaming him. There was some reason, you never knew what, maybe he *was* married, but to this day you've never blamed him.

Poor Mum. She was so shocked at first, but in time she took it all so well and helped bring up the baby Jeremy. And then you got the job in the corner shop. And it all looks, doesn't it, like a dreary, one-parent, sad-little-flat-in-town affair. And it isn't — you tell them, it isn't. Don't listen to them, girl, you're a success. For Jeremy is such a kind and earnest boy. He's gone to college (International Politics at Aber indeed) even if you didn't. And even then it wasn't you pushing him. There are plenty of women, your age and older, with sour faces and pursed lips, who drive and drive their kids, and you are damn sure that many of their sons and daughters aren't nearly as attentive and generous as your Jeremy, who is here every vacation, and proud, yes *proud*, to be seen out with you, his beautiful elegant Mum. And people can't believe he's your son, you look so young, and so the sourpusses gnash their teeth and say, She shouldn't be stuck away, serving in a corner shop, girl of her ability. And because, God knows why, Mr. Rogers called his shop the Candy Store (when in fact he's an off licence, newsagent and grocery), they call you sometimes the Queen of the Candy Store. It's derisive of course, partly because they know you can handle words like "derisive", which is an English-History-Scripture word. But it's envy as well. No-one, like no-one, is calling you a tart, and that really is the point, isn't it? For you are not only pretty, you are elegant, you are unruffled.

Look at this breakfast table, for example. It's elegantly and neatly laid, just for your own pleasure. Even a napkin. How many sourpusses have napkins at the breakfast table? Grapefruit segments, poached egg on toast, black coffee. Next week, Jeremy will be home again and you'll do him bacon, egg and tomato and you'll still be unfussed and will stride briskly in to the Candy Store by nine.

It's only quarter-to-eight now, so you can savour dressing yourself. You did in fact win a beauty contest once. When you were thirty-one, remember? And they all said, God, what is she thinking of, beauty contests, woman of her age, why doesn't she do an Open University degree or something?

Sure, they know you could. You can cope with a lot of things. You're a Friend of the Museum (the secretary, no less), you're a principal with the local operatic society — *and* (and here's the corner shop angle) before the National and the Gold Cup and before rugby matches you can discuss form in detail with the punters.

And now the sleeveless blouse. That of course is the subtle part. A floozy would go for cleavage, but you're too cool for that. Your arms are slender and tanned, and your skin is so smooth. It's a turn-on, and the punters admire you. The cool, bright heroine.

You were a heroine in 1967, weren't you? In those weekends

when Bomber had gone home on leave, you'd still go to the dance in the Masonic. And all of them had marked you down as the prettiest girl in town, all of them, and they wanted to dance with you. You liked it, you loved it, their admiration of your looks, but you were staying cool. You were staying pure for Bomber, you were Bomber's girl, pure and aloof.

Twenty-past-eight. Half-an-hour nearly in hand.You'll play tapes now, won't you? Even as you were walking proud and nude you were anticipating the moment you'd play your tapes and dream of Bomber. It's your ritual, these early mornings. If you're forty and it's 1991, people would expect sixties songs, which they're not.They're thirties and forties numbers mainly, and they were playing them in the Masonic in the 1960s. In the Mood, It Had to Be You, ballroom stuff. For you and Bomber had the most lovely ballroom summer, the most beautiful romance. And now it's twenty-to-nine, you'll need to leave in ten minutes, but yes, go on, risk it. Yours and Bomber's favourite: "Smoke Gets in Your Eyes".

"Bomber" was a funny nickname for him. His real name was Jeremy, like the son you've named after him. Because he just wasn't the "Bomber" type. Maybe that nickname too was derisive. He was a sad, warm boy, perhaps a little lost and lonely in the Forces, and you just wanted to care and care for him. So there must have been a *reason* why he didn't come back. But you're not going to blame him and you never have.

The tape ends. Smoke Gets in Your Eyes. Difficult not to cry, really. For you have, you've kept yourself for him all these years.

Ten-to-nine. Okay, world. The Queen of the Candy Store is coming...

ENTERTAINING SALLY ANN

I doubt very much if you're going to believe this. Husband, in early middle age, is instructed by wife and mother-in-law to pick up an attractive girl of twenty-four at the airport and to drive her back to Pembrokeshire. He has particularly strict instructions not to be back until well on into the second day, so is earnestly requested to spend a night with the girl in an exclusive country hotel in Powys (all expenses paid by mother-in-law).

Do me a favour, you say. This is middle-aged fantasising gone berserk. But hear me out. To appreciate the situation, you need to know more of the curious relationship between Gwyndaf, the dreamy historian, and his wife Cynthia, the latter being much abetted in all things by her mother, they two being specialists in the silvery laugh.

Cynthia and Mother-in-law are very much a part of what is known in Wales as the crachach. Their lives revolve around the Hunt Ball and similar well-oiled social functions, for which reason Mother-in-law has always looked on Cynthia's marriage to Gwyndaf as a low-key social disaster. Gwyndaf is on the one hand an Oxford graduate, which is something, but remains obstinately a history teacher, a rather un-crachach-like occupation. Moreover, his Gwendraeth Valley origins have left him with a dismissive lack of regard for social nicety, the ability barely to tell a red wine from a rosé, and a penchant for spending his leisure hours browsing in the deeper recesses of the history of Tudor Wales. Repeated efforts by Cynthia and Mother-in-law to buoy up Gwyndaf's social being have foundered on the bedrock of the historian's stubbornly dreamy and preoccupied nature. Cynthia's idea of social life is one of sparkling tinsel, a background against which she can ring out a silvery laugh and simulate flirtations with eligible young and not-so-young men ("eligible", in this case, encompassing solicitors, accountants, men in business, but not history teachers). It is all very harmless — dare one say it is a little vapid? — but it is a way of life in which Cynthia has been both groomed and, later, supported, by the peals of silvery laughter echoing back from her mother.

It is March, and diaries are being checked. Cynthia and Gwyndaf's mother-in-law have a problem. Mother-in-law has a friend, an old boarding-school-in-Berkshire friend, who emigrated many years ago to the U.S.A. and lives now in one of the grander suburbs of St. Louis. The friend's daughter, Sally Ann, a single girl in her mid-twenties, has long harboured a desire to visit Wales, so mother-in-law has said she absolutely must come to Pembrokeshire to stay with them. Fine. Girl due at Heathrow early on the morning of Tuesday the 6th of May. Right on cue, Gwyndaf is due to drive back that day from London, where he will have been attending a conference of history teachers. But only in mid-March does mother-in-law realise that she and Cynthia are away in early May, making up a little party which is spending a few days in Ireland. They are due back mid-morning on Wednesday the 7th. This will never do. Mother-in-law absolutely must be there to receive the girl. It would be possible for Gwyndaf to entertain the girl overnight in his and Cynthia's house, but people do talk, of course, and such an arrangement could give rise to the most unseemly gossip. The trip to Ireland is too, too tempting to be put off. What is to be done?

"Suppose", says mother-in-law ruminatively, "suppose that Gwyndaf were to bring the girl back rather slowly?"

"Slowly?" says Cynthia. "Mother. Gwyndaf drives slowly, I know, he dithers at junctions, but even Gwyndaf can't take a day -and-a-half to get down from Heathrow."

"Darling," says mother-in-law. "A sight-seeing journey. He could show her sights, the English countryside, he could entertain her. And we could book them into a hotel a little out of their way. Powys somewhere. That's about a hundred miles north of the motorway. Yes. Some nice little country club in Powys. I know a couple. That's what we must do."

"Mother," says Cynthia. "Gwyndaf will be furious. He hates entertaining people. And really, Mother, he can be so gauche, so awful. Gwyndaf can be awful in hotels. Usually he doesn't tip at all, and at other times he tips too much. He gets his orders muddled and confuses people. He really will hate it."

"That's as may be, darling. But Gwyndaf will have to swallow his scruples."

A meditative pause, before Cynthia giggles into gentle, inquisitive life. "Mother. What if Gwyndaf flirts with her? Outrageously, let us say?"

Mother eyes her amusedly. "Darling. Really. Gwyndaf?" They giggle delightedly. Exeunt both, to peals of silvery laughter.

And so it is arranged.

II

He looked at me in a shy kind of way and said, "You must be Sally Ann."

"That's right," I said. And, Hey, I thought, he's nice. He had a nice deep voice and that sort of silvery-grey hair around the temples you get with guys around forty. He wasn't very smartly dressed, he had an old sweater and denims, but he looked like a scholar, with glasses, a deep, calm, soothing voice and a gentle smile. And I remember thinking, as we left the airport, This is an English gentleman.

Then, later, when he was telling me how to pronounce his name, with a "v" sound at the end of "Gwyndaf", and I noticed the rather nice, funny lilt in his voice, I thought, No, he's a Welsh gentleman. Not like the English ones you get in the movies, sharp, neat guys mostly, but a nice, dreamy, gentle sort of gentleman, in denims and a sweater. I figured I might enjoy our little trip.

I knew we were going down to Pembrokeshire over a day-and-a-half, which had seemed a little funny when Mom first told me, but she'd said distances seemed much farther in the U.K. And before long, Gwyndaf took the car off the highway and I saw what Mom had meant. We were traveling through these lovely fields and villages and pasture and farmland, and Gwyndaf, my gentleman friend, was telling me all about the buildings. Now who would have thought of that? A guy drives you in his car and he talks about the buildings you pass. But the big thing was that a whole lot of these buildings are what are called mock-Tudor (and they were cute, I liked them), but Gwyndaf said come tea time (and he really did use that phrase: "tea time"), come tea time, we'd be in Shrewsbury and he'd show me some regular Tudor buildings. He was into Tudor things, he told me, he was a historian, for God's sake. Alright, I thought, not every girl gets to be driven round by a Welsh historian.

Then I think I worried a while. What did he think of me? I figured he'd find me attractive, that's no problem. I mean, I'm not too bad to look at. I weigh round a hundred and forty pounds, just a little big maybe, but my hair is long and smooth and is a nice chestnut kind of color. I have quite a good body, nice firm boobs and my hips are round and good. Okay, I'm just a little big, but I'm quite nice to look at. And, come on, it's not just looks. I think I have a nice personality.

Then Gwyndaf told me we'd be stopping at Oxford. We'd have lunch — "a meal", he called it — and then look at some of the colleges. And then he told me he'd been at one of these colleges himself. Then I really did worry. Would I be smart enough to keep this guy happy for a day-and-a-half? I'm a graduate, okay, but with a business degree from a college in Webster Groves, Missouri. And this guy was a graduate of Oxford University. But then I thought, Well no, what the heck, I majored in business admin and I'm holding down a job as a buyer with a big department store in St. Louis. I can be smart as well as nice.

And then we got to Oxford. We had lunch and then we walked round a few colleges. We went to Gwyndaf's old college, Jesus College, and hey, he knew the janitor (or porter, he was called), this incredibly old guy in what he called the lodge out front, and they kidded back and forth for a while (well not really "kidded" — they were quite grave and nice) and then we went out into this really great quadrangle, with its lawn and all these cute little staircases leading off to the rooms and studies. Only as soon as I thought that, I checked myself. "Come on, Sally Ann," I thought, "you can't think words like 'cute'. That's a real loud, brash American kind of thing to say. This is Oxford University, and the buildings are just so lovely to look at." And they were. How many people get to be shown around a lovely old college like that by a guy who's a graduate there?

Then we went on and looked at other colleges and buildings, and he told me what parts were the oldest and which were the Tudor ones. Wadham College was a Tudor one, I remember. This Tudor was obviously a big thing with him, and that was good, because I minored in British and American lit in college and I knew something about the Tudors (like about Henry Eighth and Queen Elizabeth) so I could keep the show going quite nicely.

And then, after a while, when we'd driven out of Oxford, it was like I was drifting off into a kind of dream. This was all Tudors and the past and countryside, and a deep dreamy voice easing me along. We drove on to Shrewsbury, through just endless fields and villages, and through some place (Evesham, maybe?) where there were apple orchards and this gorgeous pink and white blossom.

And then we got to Shrewsbury, at tea time. And we really did have tea, lemon tea, in a little quaint old place called a "tea room". But it seemed like Gwyndaf was busting a gut to get me back out into the streets in Shrewsbury and to show me more buildings. He was an eager kind of a guy that way. Which was nice, it really was.

Now Shrewsbury has these really wild Tudor buildings. The mock-Tudor ones we'd driven past earlier, back in Berkshire or some place, they were quite elegant, but these were... as I said, wild. They were as if they were damn near crumpled up, all squished in around the rooves, and leaning over. This was the real past now, this was really good. And... oh, there were so many other things he had to show me. There was the old town clock... and hey, I thought I had something there. One of our set texts when I minored in lit was Henry Fourth, Part One, and there's a line there about Shrewsbury clock. And that really excited Gwyndaf when I told him (like, you could see him thinking, Gee, this girl is smart), only it turned out that this was a later clock. Gwyndaf fixed the date on it, later than Shakespeare, by reading off the Roman numerals, the way these guys do.

And then we walked beside the river a while, and watched guys rowing. There's some grand kind of a school there, I guess, and guys go on to Oxford and the other old university, Cambridge,and row there.

Then, later, around six, we crossed the border into Wales (only it was odd, because we crossed it, then went back into England for a while, then crossed it again). And this was Powys, this was Wales, and we'd be stopping soon for the night.

I don't think that Gwyndaf had been to that hotel before, but it turned out to be an old Tudor mansion, so he was excited right away. He was very relaxed now and happy, and that made me happy too, because I thought, Well, he can't find me too bad to be with. We sat in the big room there, by this big crackling log fire,

and he had a good snoop round at the paintings in the room, portraits mainly. Portraits were fashionable with the Tudors, he told
me.

Then a bartender came round to our corner and said there'd be
some dancing in the dining room that night. The dining room had
a little ballroom area and a combo was due in that night, three
guys, a pianist, a bass man and a drummer. And we thought, Wow
(like, both of us thought that), Wow, let's go for it. I had a ball
gown packed away in my small valise, and Gwyndaf said he'd
packed a suit for dinner, so that was great. We chatted and I asked
him if he was a regular dancer, which he wasn't, but neither was
I, so we figured we'd shuffle round together. And then we were
off to change for our dinner-dance.

I was glad I had that ball gown when I met him at dinner. It's
not too low in front (for I'd have hated him to think I was cheap),
but it leaves my arms and shoulders bare. My arms and shoulders
are my best feature, I guess. I have a nice smooth skin and people
have commented on how nice I look with my shoulders bare.

Then, at dinner, Gwyndaf said something that puzzled me. He
said he wasn't very good with people in hotels. I couldn't see that.
With all the other people we'd met that day, like the old porter in
Jesus College and even the people in the tea room at Shrewsbury,
he'd been fine — happy and natural. But he said now he didn't
know much about wines and stuff like that, except he did know
you had white wine with poultry and red wine with red meat, and
that was all. So, we were having beef, so what say we asked for
red wine? That seemed fine by me.

Afterwards, I danced close to him. Not too close (as I say, I did-
n't want him to think me cheap or slinky — for I'm not). It's just
that it had been a lovely day, and he was a real Welsh gentleman,
and I wanted him to know I felt warm and nice about him. So just
now and again I nuzzled up against him a little. Not too often, just
now and again. A girl knows how to judge these things.

And the last thing was, just after midnight, we separated in the
corridor leading off to my room. And he took my hand (can you
believe this?) and he squeezed it just a little, then he raised it to
his lips and gave it a very gentle kiss. That really was too much.
I was very close to tears. What a lovely courteous thing to do.

In my bedroom, I lay awake a long while, watching the moonlight shine through a gap in the curtains. After a while, I got out of bed, and opened the curtains and peeped out. There was a warm lovely moonlight streaming down and all underneath were mountains and Powys and Wales. And then I went back to bed and fell asleep, dreaming of my lovely Tudor gentleman.

III

Even as we were getting introduced, and I said I was "Gwyndaf" and not "Gwyn-daff", I sensed we'd get on well together. She was a bright and cheerful girl, she'd read a little Shakespeare, and she really did make me feel that taking her round Oxford and Shrewsbury had been the right thing to do.

And of course, my vanity — and maybe it wasn't just my vanity — was touched, because she really was a beautiful woman. Or "beautiful" to my taste — to a Tudor taste, if you like. She belonged in a different and more gracious age, before our present saturnalia, and slinky little floozies. She belonged to a time when women were thought of best if they were considered "handsome" — or "comely" even. I suppose the bare shoulders revealed by her ball gown were at odds with the Tudor fashion for ruffs and high necklines, but that ballroom was no place to be pedantic. In her ball gown she was a picture. Her shoulders were bare, save for the lovely chestnut tresses flowing over them. Her arms too were bare and just slightly plump. She was a very handsome girl and it was a pleasure to be with her.

There is just the one intriguing little postscript. A day or so after Sally's and my return, Cynthia and Mother-in-law quizzed me about our trip. They conceded that Oxford and Shrewsbury had been quite good choices, and seemed deeply relieved that I'd ordered a red wine to go with the beef. Then mother-in-law hopped into life.

"And what about the country club? Was it one of their ballroom evenings?"

"Oh, yes."

"You danced with her, I hope?" said Cynthia. "You didn't leave her sitting out like a gooseberry?"

"Oh, no," I said. "We danced. Right through, in fact. To close of play, as it were."

Mother-in-law muttered approval. "Well, it seems to have paid off. The girl can't speak too highly of you. She told me she had a lovely trip." They both nodded at me, bemusedly, as if still a little baffled at my social coup. "Well done, Gwyndaf," said the perplexed mother-in-law.

Well done. My mind was far away: on Oxford, Shrewsbury, Tudor buildings, apple blossom at Evesham, Powys in the moonlight, a crackling log fire and bare white shoulders. Well done indeed.

THE MAID OF THE MOUNTAINS

I used to get irritated when he called me "Mrs. Bevan". I insisted after a while that, like everybody else, he called me "Gwyneth". I know that I was old enough to be his mother, but I found that faintly professional air of his a little off-putting.

Names and what we make of names seemed to figure prominently in our early relationship. He'd introduced himself to the staff at the bank as "Michael" and that again was in keeping with the rather heavy air he projected of being an up-and-coming professional, a well-manicured manager in the making. Before long, everyone called him "Mike", since our staff felt more comfortable that way. But I think it took him rather a while to get used to the Mike and Gwyneth idea.

He'd graduated the summer before and came to our bank as a trainee manager, a sort of rapid promotion route they have these days for the brainy. No doubt he would move in time to the obligatory Rover or Ford Sierra, but in those few months he was with us in Fishguard he was still taking driving lessons, so I used to drive him the thirty miles back and fore to work. I have just a tiny suspicion that the thought of being driven to work by a rather slaphappy middle-aged cashier went against the grain a little, and I had to jolly him along in the early days.

Having said which, I really didn't mind. He was nice. He was a well-set-up boy, nice-looking, with a clean, well-scrubbed look (although I'd happily have passed over the shaving lotion) and he had lovely black wavy hair. Best of all perhaps, he had just that tinge of seriousness and solemnity which makes boys in their early twenties so attractive. Most women of my age, let's face it, are suckers for nice-looking boys of that age, with a shy and serious side.

Something I did find disquieting though were the references to his girl friend. She, I gathered, was another professional; he even used the phrase "professional woman" once or twice. Other times, it would be "my girl friend" — once, rather alarmingly, "the Mrs." Only after quite a while did I root out the information that her name was Emma. A schoolteacher, he told me, and a B.A., not a common-or-garden B.Ed. (this being, it seemed, some profound professional distinction. Hallelujah). The crisp, professional Emma, then, was teaching back in Cardiff, whither Mike went to visit every weekend. I formed the impression of a very earnest young woman indeed, as well-scrubbed in fact as the earnest Mike, but suddenly, on into October, I got a little confidence from him which set a few alarm bells ringing. He'd referred to a couple of floodlit football matches he'd watched in town on weeknight evenings, and this was clearly something he'd enjoyed. So I asked him if he ever watched matches in Cardiff (assuming they must have even bigger and better games up in the capital). And then his features clouded slightly and I spotted that rather nice little wrinkle of a frown around his eyes. "Not often, no," he said. "To be honest, my girl friend doesn't really approve of me going to football matches. And there's often a lot of shopping to do."

And I thought, Wow. You're twenty-two, boy. You're not even engaged. Go easy. Read about the New Man, be serious, be earnest, be well-meaning, fine, but let's have a little devil too. And I suppose that from that point on I started to build up a picture of girl friend Emma, the smooth, hard-nosed professional, and I started to worry for him. Not, of course, that it was any of my business whatsoever.

Whereupon, on cue really, Becky entered the frame. Becky's my niece and she's a sweetie, a pretty, blonde, bubbly little girl, just knocking on eighteen when all this happened. She's also a leading light in our operatic society (I'm the director), and I'd cast her as Teresa in the production of "The Maid of the Mountains" we were putting on in the week before Christmas. The part of Teresa really calls for a pretty girl of the dark and gypsy-ish variety, but in local operatic societies, of course, you work with those you've got, and Becky, besides being pretty, if not dark, is a nice untutored sweet soprano. So she was to be Teresa. Then, rapidly, two things happened. Our rehearsal accompanist was taken ill and needed replacing. Then I gathered from something Mike said that he was a very proficient pianist. Fine. I roped him in.

So what does Becky do? She takes one look and she falls for him. And, as I've said, I could see why. He was a fine-looking boy. But hell. Whatever my prejudices against the absent and imagined Emma, I had to concede that he was spoken for. So when I could see Becky chatting him up in the rehearsal break (and, come on, she was giving him the full treatment: the shy glance, the demure downwards look, and then the well-timed bubble of delight), then I thought, Oh no, my girl, you're pushing it. "Becky, you little bugger," I said to her afterwards, "he's spoken for."

She sulked (a theatrical sulk, in fact; she's not theatrical really, she's not too bad, but she's a pretty girl and the usual wiles have come naturally over the years). "Come on Auntie Gwyn," she said. "I'm just being friendly. And anyway, he's not engaged or anything. He doesn't live with her." And how did she find that out, I asked myself. And then I thought, What the hell. I'd relax a little, see how the friendship went. Maybe Mike had a fifty-five-year sentence to serve with a professional wife, so maybe a little bubble and bounce with Becky as a prelude would give him a few fond memories to enliven his darker moments.

You'll gather, from the fact that I was thinking in terms of that kind of quip, that I was taking it lightly for the moment. Becky and he were nice together — and nice to each other. I could see why she liked him, and I'm sure that Becky would have an appeal for any red-blooded 22-year-old. She's a cuddly blonde of the nicest kind, pretty and funny and lively. Go for it, I felt. Gather ye rosebuds while ye may...

And then, post-rehearsal one evening, I remembered the rest of that quotation: "...old Time is still a-flying".Precisely so. That night Becky had been singing beautifully. In fact, her singing in early rehearsals had been a little held-in and tame; once Mike appeared, it became warmer and nicer very rapidly. She's no operatic star, and never will be, but she has that sweet local-operatic sort of voice, with a natural overlay of sentiment. It could have cracked Mike up, I felt. And then, come the break, they chatted happily over their Coke and I sensed something new in Becky now. Still we got the bubble and demureness mingled, still the man-catching skills of quite a high order, but something else also. I can't identify a specific gesture which was different, but I just had the feeling, as I glanced their way from time to time, that it really was genuine. This was liking, good and strong. I wouldn't say it went further than that for the moment — but what's wrong with liking, good and strong?

And hence my quotation: "...old Time is still a-flying". Back there in Cardiff was Emma, the professional woman, the praying-mantis. And here in town was the pretty Becky — not the special Becky, not the unusual Becky, just a normal, nice, happy girl. Couldn't he see the genuine article? I'm not saying he should have fallen for Becky, or married her, or anything. I just wanted to know why a nice, kind boy like that (and by this time, two lifts a day, five days a week, for over a month, I'd seen and appreciated this nice, kind side to him) could throw himself away on a female vulture who'd drag him away from his football even before they married. (Afterwards, maybe, that's for the future, things change, but women shouldn't do things like that when they're twenty-two). Let go, boy, I thought. Have a fling. Enjoy Becky and her company,and maybe you'll think again about the ominous Emma. As you'll gather, it was all a little mixed up.

Then something very interesting happened. One Wednesday morning (we rehearsed on Tuesdays and Thursdays), Mike said, as we drove to Fishguard, "Becky always dresses very nicely, doesn't she?" Yes, I agreed, urging the idea along. Yes, she does.

He seemed to muse. "It's not classy dressing... well, how shall I put it? There's the sort of smart clothing a professional woman would wear..." (Oh, shit, I thought, back to Emma again), "... but if you're out at an evening rehearsal, you dress casually, of course." (Oh dear, I thought, aren't we pompous? But go on, boy, go on). "If you notice Becky, she's always very plainly dressed, a white blouse or pullover, say, and denims usually, but she's always got these nice bright scarves and cravats." He seemed to blush and get very self-conscious. "Well, it's as if the plain clothes set off that patch of colour. Do you see what I mean?"

Wow, I thought, Whoopee. Now, boy, you're gaining. Because that, as a description of dress sense from a boy of twenty-two, was pretty good. Becky does dress exactly so, the faded blue and white, the little splash of brightness at the neck, and yes, it is natural dress sense. My own kids dress like unmade beds, so I can appreciate Becky. She's a smart girl, she's a natural. Bang on, Mikey boy.

There was of course one other angle I certainly wasn't going to tell him about. Becky has a slight scar just below the chin, after an accident, a burn, when she was a small girl, and she's always been rather conscious of it. She got into trouble in school sometimes for trying to cover it, and I think she appreciates her job in the building society now partly because of the high-necked uniform the girls wear there. And of course, always now, in civvies, she'll wear cravats or scarves at the neck. But that doesn't quite alter the fact that she does use bright colours very deftly against a plain background.

So by now I was really hoping. Maybe he'd actually start going out with Becky properly, or maybe just take the hint that we live on a planet with pretty, bubbly girls around, as well as hard-necked professional women. And maybe he'd break off the relationship with the dragon. (Had I by now caricatured Emma in my mind? I suppose I had, yes). But there were other, more gloomy moments, notably on the morning when he commented that Emma's tastes in music were a little more serious than light operetta, but she had expressed the hope (the bitch) that Mike was finding "The Maid of the Mountains" amusing. Amusing, my bum. And Becky and I were amusing also, presumably. Professional Michael down in the country, patronising the bumpkins.

There was also the morning we returned to the matter of bright coloured scarves and plain clothes. This was prompted chiefly by Becky's having appeared the night before in a very dashing new Japanese-style number, and represented a perhaps rather clumsy attempt on my part to get back to a promising area of discussion. (It was an uneasy conversation, because I had the impression that he'd been telling Emma about Becky and her coloured scarves; I was left to guess at Emma's reaction). Emma, confided the boy, hardly ever wore jeans, even on off-duty occasions. Her idea of casual wear was a neat trouser suit. But then of course, said he, she had to keep up a position as a professional woman. And of course, when he said things like that, I really hated him — I thought he was a nasty little shit. And because, underneath, he sounded shy and uncertain in saying these things, I would forgive him.

And then we came to the week of the production. A dress rehearsal with orchestra, and a four-night run, at all of which Mike was present. Becky was still in scarves, because of course Teresa in "The Maid of the Mountains" is a gypsy-girl sort of part. He'd come backstage to see us, they'd chat and bubble on, and at our last-night party he and Becky danced and talked together all night. It was a nice friendship by that time, it was warm and it was sweet.

Meanwhile, back on the morning lifts to Fishguard, there was talk of Christmas time. Mike was going back to Cardiff, of course, but would be back in town shortly afterwards. And then, on January the second, the evening before the return to work, we'd have Becky's eighteenth birthday party, a family do in my sister's house, and one to which Mike was very naturally invited. And then came the conversation in which Mike must have said he'd like to come, but Emma would be spending a few days in town between Christmas and the New Year, with an aunt or some-body, so could Emma come to the party as well? "Well," said Becky to me, "I said of course she could." And I could see her thinking, "Shit."

In the event, I got to the party very late. A couple of the kids had 'flu and Gerald was late getting back from a protracted ben-der at the golf club. So I got there around eleven, for Becky to answer the door to me. She looked tense and she looked strained — close to tearful. She was wearing a plain grey trouser suit and a coloured scarf I hadn't seen before, an orange and cream affair. For a moment, she plucked at it a little uneasily. "It's a present from Emma," she said. And then she led me in.

I was introduced to Emma. And what do I say? She wasn't too far from my mental caricature of her. Her friends would have called her elegant, which I suppose she was. Others might have used the word "aquiline". It's a measure of the nastiness I'd built up about her in my mind that I settled for "equine". She did strike me as horsey — but of course I was biased. She was tall, with neatly waved dark brown hair. She was wearing a very classy trouser suit and a quite gorgeous orange and cream neck scarf.

That is the point, of course. She'd clearly bought two, one for Becky and one for herself. Hers was silk, if ever I've seen it, it was a lovely piece. And only when Becky's scarf, in very similar colours, was seen alongside Emma's, did one fully realise what a cheap and nasty piece of Taiwanese trash Becky's new scarf was.

So why did Becky carry on wearing it through the evening? Because she was transfixed, I think. I'd thought of Emma initially as "horsey", but now the word "snake" crept into my mind. Her eye was bright and sharp, her voice clear and precise and, as we chatted, poor old Becky seemed hypnotised and helpless.

Before I could really collect myself and gather my resources sufficiently to get really catty — and I would have done, very gladly — it was time for Emma and Mike to go. "Tomorrow is in-service training," said Emma. "The professions make their demands, I'm afraid. Are you coming, Michael?" And Mike awkwardly (and unhappily, I'm sure) shuffled about, nodded faintly to Becky, and said, "Good night, all." And they were gone.

I couldn't really comfort Becky that night, but have tried to since, of course. In fact, she's rallied fairly quickly. She's a lively, cheerful girl. But that night, oddly, as I lay in bed, my thoughts were of Mike.

I was bitter at first, naturally, for the hurt he'd inflicted on Becky. And then I thought, No, not really, that's not entirely fair. He's young, he's twenty-two for God's sake, and he's got some half-baked idea about professionals — but don't we all get half-baked ideas sometimes? It's just that this one is leading him into a howling clanger and an enormous marital horror. He is so blind that he can't see the simple, lovely reality (and surely, for men, it is a reality?) of romance — of dusky gypsy maidens and cuddly blondes.

Poor sod.

ON MERLIN'S HILL

I

It is four a.m. and it is Midsummer Night. It *is* night, and around and outside my house it's dark, but it is the kind of darkness which is already stirring and warming slightly with the glow of very early morning.

Virginia Woolf, in a prose piece I most vividly remember, described the night around an Oxford college as "warm pasturage" and tonight has that sort of feel for me. It *is* pasture: a deep warm pasture in which dreams and images can be cropped and grazed.

My house is on top of Merlin's Hill, in a quiet market town in West Wales. From the kitchen window, as now, I can look out on Merlin's lane, for the moment still and hushed, but before too long, and around six, Nancy will be out exercising her dogs. Then we'll have the first of the milk floats and then the paperboy, and the lane will be back to the rhythms of a normal day. For the moment, however, I can only wonder on the odd translucence of a darkness that isn't quite darkness, and can look back and savour the strange texture of this exciting and uneasy night.

I took part in a reading tonight, at Aled Ifor's home in Aberystwyth, and drove back over the Preseli mountains at around one o'clock. Even then, the darkness wasn't quite darkness. Even at one, in the softness of mid-June, the hillsides had a haunted feel.

Even the reading itself was deliberately conceived as a Midsummer Night's Reading (for Aled Ifor has a sense of the dramatic) and the whole event seemed to have a charmed and exotic quality. We read in the garden of his quite gracious home looking down on Cardigan Bay, and the main drink on offer was a very good red wine.

I am a poet, I am forty-five years of age, and I returned to Pembrokeshire (and to Merlin's lane) five years ago, after my divorce. The fifteen years of my marriage seem now like a nightmare, something chill and threatening, enacted on the cold hillsides of Academe. Sonia was, like me, an academic, but most certainly not a poet. After her affair, when I felt myself free to go, she claimed that I was too introspective, dreaming forever of poetry and Pembrokeshire.

And now, of course, I am at one with poetry and Pembrokeshire. Lately, I have also a new female friend. Her name is Jenny, she's a widow of my own age and she teaches in a primary school. She's kind, attractive, warm and sympathetic. We go to the theatre together, to pubs occasionally, and often (as we shall today — only today is still a long way off — it's still Midsummer Night), often we'll go shopping together in Carmarthen, near to home, but just far enough away for us to be, for an afternoon, happy and anonymous among the crowds. I find a deep and soothing relief, after so long in Academia, in the easy open humour to be found in wandering the centre of Carmarthen and its market, hand in hand with Jenny. Quite possibly we shall marry in time.

To the south, on the side away from Merlin's lane, my house looks out from the top of Merlin's Hill, to fields and farming country. Now, already, a sweet red light is spreading on the hillsides.

The reading in Aled Ifor's garden was a most elegant affair, populated by scholars and research students. As I read, I was suddenly aware of, and then intrigued and captivated by, the presence of a girl of perhaps twenty-two. She gazed at me, gazed away, seemed to be actually gazing at my poems. She was extremely attractive.

It was the easiest thing, after the reading, as we mingled and chattered, over glasses of (very good) red wine, to chat to her. I was intrigued still by her gaze. It seemed an odd mixture of gentleness and scepticism. She seemed indeed a creature of half-smiles and the inscrutable.

"I enjoyed your poems," she said, "and admired them. They're very sad, aren't they?"

I agreed that, yes, they were quite sad, and almost went on to tell her that I had been hoping lately that I might write happier poems now. That seemed, however, to be too naive a sentiment for the setting and the occasion. It didn't fit with the scented almost ethereal quality of the trees and shrubs rustling behind us in Aled Ifor's garden on Midsummer Night.

"Do you read much poetry?" I asked.

"Yes," she said. "I enjoy poetry. I'm researching on Yeats."

Suddenly, but delicately, she pressed on conversationally to something which she, and not I, had known all along.

"I must admit to coming to this conversation forewarned. I believe you knew my mother once. Helen Brownjohn. You were friends, in Exeter." She paused very slightly. "She sends her love."

And suddenly the whole night and evening were lurching with excitement. Yes. Helen and I were students together... and lovers — and then she'd left for America, and we'd lost touch. Twenty-three years ago. So... God. Was this girl my daughter?

I think she'd read my thoughts — even anticipated them. "She went to America after Exeter, of course. She stayed a year, post - doctoral." She smiled. "I'm not a native American, though I was conceived there. I was born about six months after she got back."

She was smiling, very softly (surely not mockingly?) but had at least delicately relieved me of any too overpowering a sensation.

"And now?" I asked.

"She's been married for fifteen years. She was a domestic person for quite a while, but she's teaching again now, in a poly-technic. She's published a little, mainly on Yeats."

I was still rather startled by her presence, and by all of the rec-ollections of Helen. This girl too had much of Helen's inscrutable tenderness. I was indeed so shaken and so confused that it was as well that she shortly moved on. "I must circulate," she said, "but, as I said... Helen sends her love." And she smiled, impishly and lightly, we shook hands, and she moved away.

Her mother and I had been lovers, certainly. And now this daughter, this ghost of the past (I didn't even get her name). I had another glass of wine, my hand trembling as I took it. Shortly afterwards, I left Aberystwyth and drove home, round Cardigan Bay and over the Preseli Hills.

Now, in Merlin's lane, it is past five a.m. Morning is arriving rapidly and the lane (and the daily life I have come to love so much) are stirring into life. Right on cue, Nancy bustles past with her two dogs, and the milk float, as regularly, is five to ten min-utes behind. The two men who go on an early shift in the milk factory are on their way down the lane. For one curious and unhappy moment, the whole business strikes me as just a shade banal. For just behind me, fading as the Midsummer Night is fading, is the wistful ache of a long past love. Jenny will be calling this afternoon; we're going shopping in Carmarthen.

And yes, that does sound banal. My Midsummer Night's Dream is all about me, in my head and in my immediate recollection — haunting, and crowded with so many memories. And yet, the strangest thing of all, with each deepening of the daylight, the dream does fade. With each new sign of the day, I warm to that day, and I think of Jenny, who is no part of the dream at all, but everything to do with the day, and I think of our coming trip to Carmarthen. Oddly, and with a happy tug of excitement, I think of Jenny, and wonder if the sensations I feel are the first stirrings of love.

II

What's the time? Nearly three, surely? I'll look at his kitchen clock. I only came out for the bathroom really, but I'll stay in the kitchen now and make some tea. I feel excited. I've got that lovely glow about me that seems to come when you wake an hour or so after orgasm and want to be by yourself a little while.

God, that was a strange day in Carmarthen. He seemed quite agitated at first and wanted to tell me all about his trip to Aberystwyth. And what a story that was. The first love's daughter, midsummer mysteries among the trees and shrubs. He was very shaken. It must have been really odd.

The mood seemed to be with him for quite a while, and then he mellowed. He was very cheerful and very bright as we circled round Carmarthen, and yet (or did I just imagine this?) there seemed to be just a little part of him which wanted to stay close to me. Not quite "clinging", that's exaggerating, but he would nuzzle up very close to me from time to time, and squeeze my hand. Usually, when we go to Carmarthen, he'll wander off on his own to the second hand book shops, while I'm in Marks and Sparks, but today he didn't. He stayed and, really, we had a lovely afternoon.

What did we do? I wonder. We spent virtually nothing. We just goofed really, like a couple of kids, ambled round the market, sat in tea rooms (we drank a lot of tea today) and watched people passing by.

And then, very suddenly, when we were about to start back, we got into my car, and he started shivering. He said he felt cold, but he was looking troubled and worried again, about meeting that girl, I think. And he said as much: "It was such a strange night. Sinister, almost." And he suddenly looked so lost and bewildered, I just wanted to be close to him. "Come here, you soft bugger," I said. "Give us a kiss." And (can you believe this?) we were there in my car, in the car park, for half-an-hour, cuddling and smooching. We were like a couple of kids. And God, I didn't care. I care so much for him, he's been so grave and gentle for so long, and I just wanted to cuddle him, in a car park or what the hell.

And then (come on now, can you believe this?) we'd cuddled, it was around five, and we went back into town, to Morris's tea rooms, and had another cup of tea. Yep. Tea. And so what? I knew then that I'd fallen in love again. And that tea was like nectar. Everything, everything about him and the place, was just so sweet.

Later, we drove back to town, and he was quiet and peaceful. He was dozing almost alongside me. Just once he stirred, and said, "The girl I mentioned, the one in Aberystwyth."

"Yes?"

"I've just realised why she seemed so eerie. She didn't just remind me of her mother. She reminded me of Sonia as well."

"Sonia? Your wife?"

"My wife. Sonia and the past, came back to haunt me." He shook his head slightly, as if he was clearing it. "La Belle Dame Sans Merci."

"Yep," I said, "I'm with the quote. I read Keats in college."

Always in the past, when we've got back from our jaunts to Carmarthen, I've driven back to my place and we've had tea. Today I just had an odd impulse. As we were entering town, I asked, "Where now?"

"Merlin's lane," he said.

Obviously, all those memories of the car park were still with us. I hadn't been in his bedroom before, but we went there very quickly. I'd thought he'd never get round to it. And, the silly thing, he was so good. We were both good. God, I was myself again, I was back where I belong.

It's so nice to be here in his kitchen now, in this lovely dreamy middle of the night. It's nearly sunrise, I've lazed here and dreamed since three. I'll go in now and have a peep at him.

My God, he's sweet. He's sleeping like a child. And hey, look at that sunrise. It's going to be a lovely day.

SARAH'S SPRINGTIME

ONE: SARAH: MARCH 1996

Sarah wondered. She was now fourteen, so surely it must be a good time to start going out with boys.

Being fourteen wasn't too bad, once you got used to it. Thirteen had been rather confusing, with all the talk of boys and the whispering. What she'd really enjoyed had been ten and eleven, but that was all over now. Now, fourteen, Third Year at Cleevesdyke Comp. Quickly, on just one corner of her desk, she used a thick Biro to mark in the message, "Sarah and Justin 4 Ever."

She was very much aware now of so many things: the recent lovely ripening of her breasts, and the down of hair between her legs. Other things she regretted. She hated her periods. They seemed so ordinary: vulgar, messy things. Did everyone really have them? Even when she'd first been told about them, at ten, she'd felt somehow that it wouldn't happen to her. Had Louise, great-aunt Louise, had periods? Sarah thought wistfully of all she'd dreamed and imagined of her great-aunt. She seemed, from those photographs, so pure, and Sarah wanted so much to be like her.

And all the time, quietly, smugly even, she was aware of Justin, two rows behind her. He fancied her, all the girls said so, and she thought, sometimes yes, sometimes no — yes, perhaps she did fancy him. There were so many little dreamy things about him: his voice was gruff and funny now, and there was a shadow of hair over his upper lip. And, as so often, she was bound to wonder (thinking of Louise's diary): would Louise have gone out with a boy like Justin? Or boys at all?

Then Marshie bustled into the room for double English, and started the usual back-chatting with Justin, who was proud now of his reputation as class clown.

"Justin, sit down, boy, and sit still, or I'll give you a damn good hiding."

"Sir, you can't, sir. You'd be sacked."

"Not a problem, boy. I won seven million quid on the lottery last week, so they can sack me or not, as they choose. And, in the meanwhile, you'll have had a good hiding. Now sit down."

Marshie was funny: a short, round, bubbly man, with a fuzz of greyish hair and bushy eyebrows. Sarah liked to listen to him and Justin tussling away. Marshie was old, fifty perhaps, or fifty-five even, and he'd once taught Sarah's Dad. And, before that, his father had taught in the school and had taught Louise. And that was puzzling, because just a few weeks earlier, in her Granny Hester's house in Gloucester, Sarah had found just a couple of pages from Louise's diary, that everyone thought had been lost. (Sarah had spent a lot of time lately, in Granny Hester's house, rooting around in Louise's old books and papers). It was clear from those diary pages (and Sarah had kept them, hadn't told anyone about them — and she planned now to look for more), clear that Louise had liked Marshie's father. "A crush", she'd called it. Sarah could only speculate. Marshie's father had been twenty-seven when Louise had been in school, so maybe. A little proud of her own daring, Sarah tried to imagine Marshie being twenty-seven, and somebody having a crush on him. Sarah had had a crush once, in the First Year, on that young music teacher, and then he'd left.

But, crushes or not, Marshie was one of Sarah's heroes now: Marshie and Justin. Those two made a lot of noise with their by-play and arguments, but there was a quieter, gentler side to Marshie too, and Sarah knew (a little proudly, perhaps again a little smugly) that he liked her. After she'd written a story which had been a send-up of a teacher she'd called "Old Boggie", he'd started to get his own back by marking her essays and stories in Greek. When she'd asked him what these symbols meant (and he must have been waiting for her to ask), he'd stayed behind after class for a couple of minutes to explain them to her. Marshie liked inquisitive pupils. Now she was the only one — she was sure she was, the only one — he marked in Greek. She'd never gone below a Beta Plus Bracket Plus, had often had a Beta Double Plus, and once — and how excited she'd been — an Alpha Minus, with that lovely little sign of the fish.

Then, after English, on the way to registration, she just waved her fingers goodbye to Justin, and didn't speak. She'd quite have liked to talk to him, but Tanya Thomas had said that the best thing with boys like Justin was to play hard to get for a while. And then the afternoon was over, and she set off on one of her trips (she went every three or four weeks) to Louise's grave, in the church-yard up on the hill.

Although her parents didn't talk too much about her great-aunt Louise, Sarah's Granny Hester from Gloucester sometimes mentioned her when Sarah went to stay: Louise as a little girl, Louise in school in Cleevesdyke. Granny Hester had obviously thought a lot of her sister, who had died in a hospital in London when she was seventeen. Often, when Sarah was small, seven or eight, and ten, Granny Hester would lay the little girl's head on her lap to brush her hair, and would say, "My dear, you are just the image of your great-aunt Louise. She was such a lovely girl." Once, Sarah had looked up, and seen a tear rolling down her Granny's cheek. And so she, and Sarah's parents sometimes, did talk of Louise — and they all of them, always commented how like Sarah was to her — but how she'd died and of what, Sarah'd never been told.

As Sarah passed the florist's on her way up the hill, she felt a twinge. Occasionally, she bought a little spray and put it by Louise's grave. (The family must have known, but they didn't really encourage it; nobody stopped her going to her great-aunt's grave, but she felt they weren't entirely happy about it — so Sarah went there quietly, occasionally, and for only short visits.) Today though, she passed the florists's by — it would have been too big a dip into her pocket money.

Louise's headstone was a marble one, and Sarah was very proud of that. Most of the headstones in the churchyard were plain stone ones, and Louise's stood out proud and tall. The family had obviously been very fond and proud of her.

Now, Sarah gazed for quite a while at the headstone. "In loving memory... departed this life, 19th October, 1945. Aged 17 years. Ever in our thoughts." It was a cold March day, and the grey, almost blue-grey clouds went blustering by in a rough wind. Sarah wondered. She thought of what she'd read in those scraps of Louise's diary. Louise hadn't liked boys, not really, although she'd dreamed once of what she'd called a "male person". Perhaps she'd never met anyone like Justin...

TWO: LOUISE: APRIL 1942

...way to celebrate your fourteenth birthday, but there was no getting out of it. I didn't for one minute want to sit with a sixteen-year-old boy cousin, looking over his stamp collection, particularly when he's as boring as Grenville. I wasn't sure which was worse, Grenville or the stamp collection.

But there's the evening over and I must tell you now, diary, of the strange dream I had last night. I dreamt I was in the High Street, Cleevesdyke High Street, walking down hand in hand with the most wonderful boy. I'm not sure even if he was just a boy. The way the dream felt at the time, it seemed as if he was just a sort of male person. And I seemed — or felt — what did I feel? I felt I was more of a woman than a girl. And the really wonderful thing was that it was night-time (I'm sure of that, even though it was a dream, because it had that excited night-time feeling) — it was night-time and yet the streets were full of light. Really blazing with light. And then I woke, and I remembered the black-out. Sometimes that is so frustrating, because I can hardly remember now walking the streets at night, and street lights. It must have ben so lovely.

I love the cinema. American films, full of street lights. Broadway and cities, big American cities with blazing lights, and the bars and cafes open until early in the morning. But that won't happen in Cleevesdyke in wartime — or ever perhaps.

Never mind. I had my dream and my street lights for a while — and my secret male person. A lovely birthday present.

Monday, 27th April, 1942.

School was quite good today. Geography was interesting for once, oddly. We were reading about deltas. Maths and Chemistry passed, and didn't bother me too much. Oh, and I did enjoy History. I do so love the Tudors — how grand and opulant (have I spelt that correctly?) — how grand it all seems. Miss Stokes passed round a book with colour pictures (yes, colour — wonderful!) of Kings' College Chapel, and she told us it was called Kings' (apostrophe after the "s", diary) because they were generations building it. Cambridge must be so fine. How beautiful it must be to live in such a grand and lovely city.

And, of course, Marshie's lesson was fun. We were reading a

poem called "John Gilpin" and it was so humorous, so funny, and it suited his voice. A lot of poems suit Marshie's voice. I really do like him. He's humorous and woolly and kind, and his big bushy eyebrows race up and down as he reads. Really (and this is a *dark secret*, I'll never tell a soul) I, like him in a special way — a way I don't like boys. The other girls would laugh and say it was a crush. I suppose it is really, and crushes are rather silly, when you come to think of it. I mean, he is absolutely aeons older than I am, somebody said he's twenty-seven. But he is such a kind and dreamy person.

And he's a mystery person too. Why isn't he in the Forces? We've all wondered, and Greta Morris heard a rumour that he had a weak heart. And could you imagine Marshie in an American film, or bright-lit streets, like my secret male person? Probably not...

THREE: JUSTIN: MAY 1996

Justin had been looking forward to today. It was going to be the day he asked Sarah to go out with him.

He'd started the morning playing football on the Rec with some of the boys. But Sarah'd told him, or more or less told him, the week before, that she went into town about ten every Saturday morning. So at about quarter-to-ten, he left his game on the Rec and dawdled along to the end of Sarah's estate.

And all the way along his walk he was musing and recollecting, his excitement growing. It was catching in his throat, it was pulsing. It was strange and happy. A girl. Sarah. She had tits now, it was obvious, and there were all the other things about girls. For most of that term, quiet sometimes even in Marshie's lesson, he'd gazed at the bra-strap under her tight summer-term blouse, and delighted in the little swelling of her breasts as she turned. The thought keep coming back, and he kept thinking: Hey, a girl.

Sarah had been away all half-term week, at her Granny's in Gloucester. He'd last seen her on the day they'd broken up, and they'd talked. For quite a while before that, it had seemed she didn't want to talk, but that Friday, looking hot and happy (they were both hot and happy) they talked.

"Might see you the Saturday you get back," he'd said.

She'd blushed a little. He'd tried to sound casual.

"You still go into town Saturdays?"

She'd nodded. "Usually. Around ten."

Then, that Saturday, as he reached the end of her estate, she was there, walking up to the end of the road. She was very dark and very pretty. She saw him, slowed, and allowed him to walk beside her. Slowly, they walked down the hill into town.

He wondered: perhaps she was waiting for him to ask her out. But things (and Sarah) moved very slowly. She seemed stiff and grumpy, not happy the way she had been the Friday before half-term. When he eventually spoke about her holiday in Gloucester, and asked her if she'd enjoyed herself, she just replied, "All right."

He tried again, half hoping, half hoping not. "Are you meeting the girls this morning?"

"Girls?"

"Tanya Thomas. Sophie. That lot."

"No."

"Oh. Sorry. I thought you might meet them Saturdays."

"Well, I don't meet them. Or I'm not this morning. I'm getting some shopping for my mother."

So they walked into town, walked round, and he waited outside Spar and the post office while she bought her mother's stamps and groceries. Slowly (and Justin's frustration was building now — he was getting fed up with this), slowly they walked back up the hill. It was nearly half-past eleven when they reached the end of her estate, which was where he'd planned to ask her out. She'd barely spoken.

"I'm glad you had a good holiday," he said.

And suddenly her face was quick and mobile, her eyes were gleaming, and wet with tears. "Well, I didn't. It was horrible. I found some old letters of my Granny's, from Louise, my great-aunt. And it was horrible, what they did to her. It *wasn't very nice.*" She pummelled, suddenly and wildly, at his chest, shouting "I hate you! I hate you! I hate you!" And she ran, back up the road and away from him.

Justin was totally bemused, and stayed, shocked and wondering, for about ten minutes. Only slowly did he cross the road, back to the Rec. Bugger it. He thought he might as well play football. He was relieved when one of the boys shouted, "Go in midfield, Justin. We're short."

After a while, his mood eased. He was back in a familiar routine now. He was angry — of course he was angry, the silly bitch — and it showed in his game. He started diving into tackles and was winning the ball every time. He dispossessed somebody with an almost contemptuous ease and strode forward, shrugging off a tackle, before driving a powerful through ball into his opponents' half.

FOUR: LOUISE: SEPTEMBER/OCTOBER 1945

10 Wye Valley Road,
Cleevesdyke,
Monmouthshire.

15th September, 1945

My dear Hester,

I'm sure it's a very defiant and even wicked thing to do, or to want, but I do so much need to write and tell you about my baby. I know Ma and Pa will have written to tell you, but I do so want to write to you myself (but I'm not telling them that I'm writing — please don't say anything). I know that what I did was wrong, but somehow I do still want to tell you myself.

Ma and Pa are being very kind really, and I know they care about me, but I feel all the time that awful sense of how disappointed and upset they both are, and then I wonder and wonder, how wrong it was. I feel something awful has happened, that I've done something really awful.

Mine is a VE Night baby, Hester, and I wonder if there are others of them. It was such a wonderful time, such excitement. They were a wonderful few days. You'll remember, because it must have been the same your way. It was marvellous, after all those war years, to have people out crowding in the streets again, the streets so full of happy, excited people. I'm sure this is quite a wicked thing to say, but mine is a celebration baby. It's shameful, I know, but I don't altogether regret what happened. Not altogether.

I suppose I should tell you about my boy friend, Allen, or perhaps I should call him my lover, although I don't really like the word "lover". It's a new sort of word really, from the films, and I

91

still prefer to say "boy friend", because he is only a boy really. He's gone back to America now, his regiment went back soon after the war. He was only twenty-one, and that isn't that old. Not really. You're only twenty-three, Hester, and you've been a married lady for nearly two years.

Of course, I do know now about Allen's wife, and I do see that it was a terribly wrong and foolish thing to have done, but please understand, dear Hester, that I didn't know then about his wife (I didn't know until he'd gone back and he wrote) and for six months Allen was so kind and considerate, so tender. Do you understand, Hester? Do please try to understand. At the time it was all so wonderful.

What will happen now I don't know. I dearly, dearly want to keep my baby, and I hope you understand that, I'm sure you will, because you'll have a baby yourself very soon, and I'm sure you must feel the same excitement as I do. But Ma and Pa think maybe the baby should be adopted.

I don't want to write any more for now. Try to understand. Please write back to me, Hester, but you'd better not mention or acknowledge this letter. I don't want to feel more disloyal and wicked than I do already.

Your loving sister
Louise.

10 Wye Valley Road,
Cleevesdyke,
Monmouthshire.

5th October, 1945

My dear Hester,

I must write, briefly and secretly, just to ask for your love and prayers. My news, I know, will have gone before me. Ma and Pa are adamant. I'll be at the clinic for just a few days and then I'll be home again. They say it's a clinic, a little clinic sort of place, run by someone Pa knew in the Army, or his wife, I think, and it's just outside London (And I think, how awful it is to say this, how much I've always longed to go to a big city like London, and now to have to go in disgrace like this). It seems a terribly long way to go, but Ma and Pa want it to be done a long way away, and then we'll tell people I went to have a cyst removed. Then (I suppose) we'll all get back to normal. But, Hester, how *can* I get back to normal with Allen gone and my baby gone?

I did ask them if it was a risk, because I'm so afraid, Hester, and they're so adamant, so ashamed of me, that I can't talk to them, or even cry to them anymore. Hester, getting rid of a baby is illegal, isn't it? It's wrong, surely. Am I being asked to do wrong? Of course, what I did was wrong. I feel so muddled.

And, of course, I'm afraid. I'm terribly frightened. Please pray for me, my dear sister. Please keep me in your thoughts.

Your loving sister
Louise
P.S. I'll be back in Cleevesdyke in just a fortnight or so. Please write to me by then.
Louise

FIVE: SARAH: JULY 1996

The sun was streaming down, and Sarah's blouse was sticking quite tightly to her chest and her back. Her last summer's blouse was a little small now, and she was very conscious of its tightness, and the way it pronounced her figure just a shade too clearly.

The buses had gone, school had been over for half-an-hour, and Sarah waited by the school gates for Justin to appear. Her moods mingled confusedly. It was the first time she'd been out with a boy properly and her parents had said she could go. The two of them were going to go from school to the Astoria Cafe down in the High Street, then back up for a walk round the Rec, then home. Sarah wondered if Justin would want to snog her, then hoped he wouldn't. Perhaps he'd kiss her, she wouldn't mind that, but "snog" was a nasty Tanya Thomas kind of word.

For a while, after her visit to Granny Hester's, she'd been very unhappy, frightened even, about herself and Justin. What had happened to Louise was terrifying, and she'd wanted to run, to hide from boys, from Justin, from all that she was feeling.

And then the sun had come out. One morning in early July, she'd woken to find the light and sun streaming into her bedroom. She'd felt her breasts rolling slightly against her pyjamas and she'd suddenly thought (and the thought had glowed happily in her mind, solving everything): Louise's soldier had betrayed her, but Justin wouldn't be like that. She'd felt, suddenly and excitedly, that it was time.

She and Justin had talked (and she'd realised that she'd been nasty to Justin that Saturday, so she'd said she was sorry) and they'd fixed their date. And then, the silly thing, Justin had got a detention from Marshie, for chopsing. He'd been very excitable that morning and had chopsed back once too often. Marshie had been annoyed by that and he'd told Justin he had to stay in till half-past-four. Now, outside the school, at twenty-five past, Sarah wondered (and perhaps this too was a little smug) if Justin had been excited because he was going out with her, and if that had made him mouthy. She kept thinking about it, feeling now rather tense. She was breathing in very hard, to stay calm, and this only made her self-conscious again about the pressure of her breasts on her too-tight blouse.

The day before, she'd gone very solemnly, not quite knowing why, to Louise's grave. ("Departed this life, 19th October, 1945"). She'd taken a spray of flowers this time. She'd puzzled about Louise, how pure she'd seemed, and about her soldier. She forgave her everything. She'd felt (an odd thing to feel with someone you'd never met) she'd felt she loved her. Louise would understand about her and Justin. Sarah had cried a little, she hadn't really known why, and then she'd put her flowers gently on the plinth, and whispered to Louise, "Goodbye".

And now Justin was out of school. He was strutting slightly, his shoulders back, swaggering a little. Boys walked like that after detention, she'd noticed.

"Shall we go down the Astoria?" he asked (and she trembled at the slight huskiness in his voice). They set off slowly.

"My old man said I should treat you," said Justin. "Gave me a couple of quid. You can have what you want."

She was pleased to find him so kind and considerate. "I'll have a Cherry Coke," she said.

Clumsily, uncertainly, partly excited — and, for just a second or so, a little afraid — she took his hand.